D1557501

Heat

Heat

Poomani

Translated from the Tamil by
N. Kalyan Raman

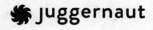 juggernaut

JUGGERNAUT BOOKS

KS House, 118 Shahpur Jat, New Delhi 110049, India

First published in Tamil as *Vekkai* by Padaippagam 1982
Published by Juggernaut Books 2019

10 9 8 7 6 5 4 3 2 1

P-ISBN: 978-93-8622-894-9
E-ISBN: 978-93-5345-038-0

Typeset in Adobe Caslon Pro by R. Ajith Kumar, Noida

Printed and bound at Thomson Press India Ltd

Contents

1

Chidambaram had only planned to hack off the man's right arm.

He was aiming for the shoulder, but instead the sickle had sliced through the upper arm, its sharp tip entering the ribs. The severed arm had dropped near his feet. He kicked it away, grabbed the sickle and fled. As he ran, he heard the man's scream rise and fade like the final cry of a goat in a butcher's yard.

Luckily, the street lights had been off the whole time. As he sprinted down the darkened main road, lit only by candles flickering in the shops, he turned back to see if anyone was following him.

He could sense a couple of men running towards him silently. Behind them, a bus had turned the corner. In the beam of its headlights, he saw the figures giving him chase.

He darted away from the light to the edge of the road. He wiped the sickle in the dirt and rubbed it clean. Dabbing the sweat off his forehead, he shoved the weapon into the sheath hanging at his waist. From a cloth bundle tucked into his waist, he took out a handmade bomb and held it ready, waiting for the bus to pass.

The shadows were drawing near. He stopped, took aim carefully and tossed the bomb. It exploded with a bang, filling the area with smoke. He began to run again with even more vigour.

No one would follow him now. As he approached a corner of the main road of the town, he dropped his speed, turned into the street that led to the cattle fairground and vanished into the dark.

His feet stumbled on heaps of garbage. He slowed down to a walk. After wrapping the two remaining bombs again in the cloth bundle, he tied it to his waist. He stopped to pee under a tree. He was no longer panting.

The bomb, which he had rigged with his own hands, had not failed him. It had exploded with the force of a jumbo firecracker. Had his aim been on target, his pursuers couldn't have returned home.

The lights were back on again. He walked through the unlit areas along the town's edge. He could hear the rumble of trucks in the match factories moving contraband loads of matchboxes in the dark.

There was the usual clatter and noise from the ginning factory. Visitors to the weekly market passed down the road, talking among themselves. Lights twinkled in the neighbouring villages as if stars had sprung up from the ground. He arrived at the foothill on the edge of the town, where their street lay.

He didn't want to go home, but he had to see Ayya. His father would scold him: 'What a stupid thing you've done, just like a little boy!'

What could he do? The matter had gone too far. They should have made Vadakkuraan walk around with an arm missing, but it had ended this way instead. No man could have survived that deep stab in the ribs. No one could feel sorry for him now.

Chidambaram reached the public tank. Tamarind trees had spread a seamless darkness over the bank. There was no sign of anyone. He squatted low, listening with an alert ear, scanning his surroundings. Avoiding the usual paths, he found a secluded spot and climbed down to the tank. He removed the sickle from his waist and rinsed it clean, washed the sweat from his neck as well as his hands and legs, and wiped himself dry. The stench of blood was gone now.

As he climbed back on to the bank with a heavy

heart and headed towards his street, a jumble of thoughts raced through his mind.

He would find Mama first and tell him about the incident. Mama would in turn inform Ayya. On the hilltop, light from the temple lamp illuminated the surroundings. Men moved about in the shadows lining both sides of the street. He stopped to watch them. Suddenly the beam of a flashlight trained on him. He signalled back by waving his towel. A few minutes later, a figure appeared carrying a spear staff.

'Who is it?'

'One of ours.'

'What do you mean, ours . . .? Ah, it's the big shot. Come, come.'

His uncle looked happy. He put an arm around Chidambaram's shoulder and led him away. A few more men stood under a neem tree. Chidambaram recognized each man.

'Why are they here, Mama?'

'We were all waiting for you – after what you've done.'

'What have I done?'

'Oh, you did nothing, eh? Then why are you sneaking around like this in the dark?'

'I had just gone out to shit.'

The men sniggered softly. Pretending to pat him on the back, Mama felt around Chidambaram's waist too. He found the sheath with the sickle inside.

'Why do you need this to shit?'

'Just for safety. Don't put your hand on that side. I have other goods too.'

'Your father was right. You do have a heart of stone, boy.'

'Where is Ayya?'

'Not here.'

'Where has he gone without you? Why are you standing here?'

'We heard that some men from Vadakkur village were coming this way. We have to see what it's about, don't we?'

'Who will dare to come here?'

'Yes, our boy has finished off the enemy. Who'll dare now?'

'Is he dead?'

'You don't know?'

'Who told you?'

'We know the whole story.'

'Does Ayya know?'

'Of course. You are his son, after all.'

Chidambaram was silent. Mama tousled his hair.

'We are just a useless bunch. We should've wiped out Vadakkuraan's entire family by now. Never happened. Instead, we drank arrack every day and loitered about. You're not even fifteen yet, but you've made us look like wimps. Now your father won't even look people in the eye; he slinks away with his head down.'

Chidambaram took hold of his uncle's hand. The other men watched them in the dark.

'Have the police turned up yet?'

'How can they come so fast? They'll wait till the wretched corpse is taken away. Let them come if they want to. We are ready.'

'If the police find out about me, they are sure to come.'

'How could they know who it was in that crowd?'

'Yes, it was a really big crowd.'

'He was cornered in a good spot.'

'I tried to trap him in two or three other places; nothing worked. He sat leaning back in a chair at the barbershop. I went in as if to comb my hair and checked it out. The place wasn't suitable. I could only strike him on the neck. The poor owner could lose his business. After the strike, it would be hard to get away. The police station is nearby. Someone or the other would be standing at the entrance.'

'Doing it there would have been a mistake.'

'I then found him in a food stall. He stepped outside after eating and lingered there, belching. But he was folding betel leaves with both hands in front of him. I had decided on cutting his arm. If I struck his leg, he would lie around at home, unable to move around, right?

'So you got him at the temple junction, finally?'

'I thought it was a convenient spot. To escape, I could run south and disappear into the cattle fairground. He bought something in the sweets stall and stood where I could strike him easily. But he stepped back just as I raised the sickle. It went into the ribs. I had a hard time pulling it out.'

'You should have left it there and run away. Never strike at close range in a crowded place. There's no telling what might happen.'

'I first thought I'd throw a bomb and take off. But if the bomb didn't explode, it'd be a mess. My plan was only to chop off his right arm and make him a cripple. So I grabbed the sickle and ran, ready for anything.'

'You tossed a bomb too?'

'I was running in panic, and these men were after

me. They were asking for trouble. I guessed they were policemen because their footsteps weren't heavy or loud. I thought they'd give up at some point, but they didn't. It was then that I threw the bomb, thinking I had to finish them off too. They were out to catch me, right? The bomb went off like a clap of thunder. Had it struck them, they would've died. I didn't know what happened. I ran circling the town, washed up in the public tank and came here.'

'They survived the bomb. Tomorrow we'll find out who they were. Why didn't you say a word to me?'

'Why should I drag everyone into trouble, Mama? Maybe I should've told you. Whenever I stood behind you, sizing up your arm, I did think of telling you. Even so, I decided against it.'

'Oh, you did that, did you?'

'Just to get an idea. You are exactly as tall as that man.'

'Your father was watching while it happened. When it was over, he came running to us, saying our cub has killed a rabbit. I didn't understand what he meant. Then he told us the whole story.'

'All the lights went out as if it had been planned beforehand. I was walking fast, with the sickle hidden inside my dhoti, and suddenly it was dark. The sweets stall owner lit a candle and fixed it on the counter.

Vadakkuraan put his hand out to collect the snack. One strike and that was it . . . Where's Ayya?'

'He said he was sending your mother away and he's asked to meet you.'

'Where is Aaththa going?'

'East. To your chiththi's village.'

'My sister?'

'Your mother is taking her along.'

'Our house?'

'We've moved the kitchen items and provisions to the headman's house; yours is now locked.'

'The dog?'

'It'll go with your father. I thought of keeping it, but it won't stay.'

'It won't stay with him either. I'll be off then.'

'Stay here tonight. I'll take care of you. You haven't eaten anything; how can you roam around hungry in the dark? Your aththai will shout at me. From the moment she heard what happened, she has been crying and asking for you.'

'I've had something to eat. Don't need anything now. Tell Aththai for me. I'll start right away.'

Meanwhile, Mama sent someone to bring Aththai.

Aththai's voice was worn out from crying. She begged him to eat. He just wanted water. She brought some from a neighbour's house. He drank the water and started out. Mama and a few others walked with him up to the public tank and saw him off. They were carrying weapons. He recognized them in the dark: Ayyanar and Karupayya, along with Kaarmegam, who was holding a staff in his lone hand.

'Do you want me to come along?'

'No need, Mama. We need men in the street too.'

Leaning his staff on the shoulder, Kaarmegam folded his dhoti up to the knee with his one arm.

'We are here. We'll take care of everything.'

'Let Mama stay back, though.'

Mama didn't refuse.

'You know the abandoned well beyond the north stream? That's where you'll find your father.'

'I'll get there. You go back.'

North of the public tank, he could make out the cart track from the ruts on the ground, but he chose not to take that route. He took the shortcut instead, through the shrubs and dead foliage. Before reaching the stream, he had twice stepped on thorns and pulled them out. A cluster of palm trees stood on the far bank. Ayya must be waiting there. He searched among the trees. He couldn't find him. Then he heard a dog whining beyond the palm trees and moved cautiously in that direction.

A man was sitting on the stepping stone beside the abandoned well. He coughed gently and cleared his throat. When Chidambaram moved closer, the dog groaned and leapt up. Ayya stroked its back to quieten it. As soon as Chidambaram sat down on the stone directly opposite him, Ayya removed the towel wrapped around the dog's neck.

Chidambaram felt suddenly too shy to speak. He rubbed the dog's neck without looking up at his father. The dog climbed on to the stone and licked his face. Its wagging tail lashed his back.

Ayya pushed the plants at the back to one side to check for intruders.

'Who told you that I was here?'

Chidambaram kept his head bowed.

'Mama.'

'Where did you meet him?'

'On our street.'

'Nothing happened there, right?'

'No. Our people are ready and waiting.'

'Why did you go straight to our street?'

'I took the path from the public tank. They were waiting for me.'

'Never mind where they were waiting; going to our street was a mistake.'

'I had to tell them what happened, didn't I?'

'Fine time to tell them, after it is all over. You should have thought of it first. You're a big man now, it seems, and it's *our* job to keep track of you. If something happened to you, what would we do? Your brother is already lost, killed in cold blood. We only have you. How can we stay alive after losing you? How shall we console Mama and Aththai? That woman will cry herself to death.'

The dog lay quiet in the kamalai[1] pit.[2]

'Why would I have got caught?'

'You'll say that, won't you? Why didn't you tell me?'

'You would've stopped me.'

'I waited for so long to kill him. You beat me to it.'

'You tried for so many years.'

'I am a coward, son. Anyway, how does it matter who did it? He killed my older boy, and now you've cut him down. And he fell writhing in front of the temple entrance like a slaughtered goat. We shouldn't have spared him for so long. He did so many terrible things in the villages around here.'

'I only wanted to see him missing an arm.'

---

[1] kamalai: cattle-driven water-lift system for drawing water from wells for irrigation

[2] kamalai pit: downward sloping pit adjoining the well for the bulls to move to and fro for drawing and lifting water from the well

'What good is that? This is the best way to settle accounts, once and for all. If he was just crippled he wouldn't have kept quiet. He would have bribed the police with all his money to keep on troubling us. We wouldn't have been able to live in peace.'

'Were you there?'

The question seemed to singe Ayya.

'I haven't become that worthless, son. I was there, keeping an eye on everything that happened.'

Chidambaram didn't speak. The dog was straining at the leash – it had smelled the field mice scurrying between the bushes around the abandoned well – and he was trying to hold it back. Ayya continued, 'I knew something was up that day. You washed your clothes. Then you visited the temple. You came back with sacred ash smeared on your forehead. Then you carried your sister to the market and bought her all kinds of things.'

'Just the usual.'

'Don't bluff. Why did you tell your mother to feed the dog early? She would have done it herself. While she was feeding the dog, you picked up a sickle and set out for the market. Something was bulging at your waist.'

'I carry it always.'

'Then why did your mother feel uneasy and tell me

about it? So I also picked up my sickle and followed you. You entered the barbershop. You lingered near the eatery. I followed, watching you. If I had passed in front of the sweets stall, it would have thwarted your plan, so I waited under the cover of the rest house. The light was bothering me. I couldn't think straight. So I ran to the transformer, fumbled around and pulled out the fuse. Your aim was on target, so I didn't join you. You ran south. I came home.'

'So it was you who put out the lights. I was surprised about the timing. I did feel nervous under the light. When everything went dark, I felt confident again.'

'I heard a bomb go off. Where did you get it from? Did Mama give it to you?'

'I put it together myself.'

'Did you? So that's why you were loitering behind the soda factory, picking up porcelain bits.'

'The other day, when you were rigging a few, I asked you for a couple of pieces. You refused.'

'From now on *I* should be asking you, it seems.'

Lights flashed on the cart track to the north. The men from Vadakkur were on their way. The light from their lanterns was advancing rapidly. He held the dog back, making sure that it stayed quiet. Ayya walked out, listened for sounds and came back.

'Are they from Vadakkur?'

'Yes, the punks who shaved his private parts for a living. They're going with the police to watch over his corpse.'

'Do they think someone's going to steal the corpse and gobble it up?'

'They are running scared.'

'What happens if the men from our street see these fellows and start a fight?'

'Your uncle will take care of it.'

'Waiting here is not a good idea.'

'I came here for a reason. How can we kill a man and go our own way? If a fight breaks out in the street, everyone will be in danger. We had to come away. If the fellows from Vadakkur approach, we can alert our men and get them ready. If something happens, we can jump in.'

'Who is going to fight for this fellow's sake?'

'Don't say that. If there's talk that we went over to their town and killed a man, there'll be trouble. Who is going to worry about why it happened? He has taken all our land and left us with nothing but our bare hands and loincloth. But are they going to think about that?'

'Let them come here if they want to.'

'They won't go back alive if they do.'

A lapwing called out two or three times. Inside

the abandoned well, the crickets had begun their loud chatter.

Both of them were sitting relaxed on the stepping stone with their legs stretched out in front of them.

'Where have you dumped the sickle?'

'I didn't get rid of it. I washed it and tied it again to my waist. I also have two bombs.'

'Will you give them to me? I'll carry them for you.'

'No, I'll keep them.'

'Any bloodstains on your clothes?'

'Don't see any.'

'Get rid of them. Here, put these on.'

Ayya took out a dhoti and shirt from his bag and gave them to him. He wore them; then he secured the sickle and the bombs at his waist.

'Did you bring a towel?'

'Mama will bring the rest.'

'Will Aaththa take my sister along?'

'Why wouldn't she? She will stay with Chiththi. She is very brave. She was born a woman, but she is more spirited than all of us.'

Light from the traffic flow on the road had decreased. Ayya was immersed in thought. Chidambaram ventured gently: 'Shall I check if Mama is on his way?'

Ayya crouched below the stepping stone, lit his bidi, concealing the flame, and inhaled deeply, covering the lit end with both hands.

'Go to the stream, wait behind the cover of a bush and look out for him.'

Chidambaram set out with the dog. Though he waited for a long time, there was no sign of his uncle. He returned to the well. He found Ayya and Mama chatting. Which route had Mama come by?

'Did you take the roundabout way, Mama?'

'I got here somehow.'

Mama pulled Chidambaram close and made the boy sit near him. Chidambaram listened eagerly to their conversation, keeping himself warm with Mama's towel.

'Feeling cold, are you?'

He watched them. First they came to a decision about money. Mama said bluntly, 'Why are you so worried about money, machaan? It's not like we can't handle it. Let's not talk about it any more.'

'That's not it, maapillai. You've faced trouble all your life because of us. Why should you continue to suffer?'

'So you think I've suffered! Won't I spend money if my boy does it? As if we can live happily after sending our only boy to jail. Even if we set all our fields on fire, will it douse our anger? Why are you talking rubbish?'

Ayya fell silent. After a while, he clucked his tongue.

'Maapillai, why should we leave our neighbourhood to go into hiding? Can't we stay on, moving between hideouts?'

'You may as well ask me why you can't stay at home.'

'Who is going to betray us?'

'It's not a good idea to be in the locality, machaan. Given our bad luck, someone will spot you. In all ways, staying out will be better. Do you want me to come with you?'

'We are not scared. Me, I can hide for months together. But we must think of Chelambaram. Come what may, we are leaving.'

'You don't have to think of him. Do it for your own sake.'

'Leave it, then. We won't step into the village till you send for us.'

'The dog won't stay back.'

'Shall we leave it with your sister?'

Chidambaram didn't like the idea. Mama didn't like it either.

'How can we take the dog that far, machaan? You

18

can't keep it with you either. Let it stay back in my house. It will be difficult, but I'll manage.'

'If you are home, you'll be able to handle it. But you also have to go into hiding for some time.'

'I'll take care of that. Don't worry.'

Going into hiding didn't seem like a big challenge to Chidambaram. He slipped in a word hesitantly: 'Why, Mama? Why should Ayya come with me? Needless trouble, isn't it? If the dog is with me, I'll manage. You two can stay here and get things done.'

Mama looked at Ayya. Ayya was staring into the dark night.

'Have I become a useless old man? Look at the way he talks.'

'Don't mistake him, machaan. He is only trying to be helpful.'

Chidambaram was embarrassed. He didn't say anything.

Finally, it was decided that Mama would take the dog with him. Mama took Ayya aside and talked with him for a long time. Chidambaram had a difficult time calming the dog and sending him away. Before leaving, Mama asked Ayya, 'Machaan, do you have all the supplies you need, or have you missed something? Should I give you what I have?'

'See, you've started talking like your nephew.'

'Fine, then. So long as you have everything you need. Take care and come back safe.'

Chidambaram stood watching till Mama, walking eastward and struggling to pull the dog along, faded into the darkness. Chidambaram had forgotten to give him the towel. Ayya picked up the bag that Mama had given them.

They did not return to that abandoned well again. It was late at night and the weather was turning cold. Both tied their towels tightly around the head like a turban, covering their ears.

The stream lay in the east like a squiggly black wick. Chidambaram walked behind his father.

2

Tuesday was dawning. Chidambaram and his father waded down a stream through a village common. People were stirring. They hurried on, worried that some villagers might also come over to the stream. As they kept walking, the stream grew wider and merged into an irrigation tank.

There was a dense growth of reed thickets in the shallow pools at the mouth of the stream. Flower clusters swayed gently amid the thickets.

Chidambaram took the bag from Ayya, and breaking off a twig from a babul tree, cleaned his teeth with it. Ayya squatted on the sloping bank to defecate, then he washed his face with water from the tank. Later, as Ayya stood waiting on the bank, Chidambaram did his morning chores.

Chidambaram was hungry. Sunlight had spread

gently on the water, but it was too cold to drink. Standing knee-high in the water eased the throbbing pain in his legs. He washed his face to shake off the vestiges of sleep.

Ayya started walking again. He could withstand hunger. Sometimes he would drink arrack on an empty stomach and roam about aimlessly. On such days, he would eat only at night. Aaththa would move about the house, complaining. 'Oh, he needs the rush more than gruel or water, does he?' she would mutter to herself as she set down each utensil as noisily as possible. Ayya wouldn't utter a word.

Chidambaram tried to stay clear of such discord. He would sneak away quietly to his uncle's house. There he sought out his aunt, who prepared food and fed him with her own hand. Then she'd spread out a mat for him to sleep on. He'd fall asleep instantly. This happened quite often.

The embankment ended at the sluice of the irrigation tank. On the other side of the sluice, the stream flowed towards the next village. As they walked, Ayya kept his eye on the trees by the tank bed in front of the sluice. He climbed down at the sluice to have a look and came back.

'What do we do for food, son?'

'I'm not hungry.'

'Let's suppose I am.'

'We have to go to a village nearby and get something.'

Chidambaram stood watching the water-worn pits on the sluice gate.

'We need money for that.'

'I have some.'

'Your own?'

'Mama used to give me a little money now and then.'

Ayya sat down on top of the sluice.

'Sit here. Let's see what your uncle has kept inside this bag.'

Ayya opened the bag. There were dhotis and shirts in the top layer. He took out a cloth bundle and opened it: a food parcel. In another cloth packet, they found salt, tamarind, chillies and onions. The rest of the bag was filled with rice.

Chidambaram had not imagined that there would be so many items inside the bag.

'So, that's why the bag felt heavy.'

'It's all your aththai's work.'

Aththai had managed to do so many things in a short time. Amid all the commotion and her own sobs and tears, she must have packed each item calmly and thoughtfully.

She would have packed the food she had cooked for her family. They must have run short that night. Given the state she was in, she couldn't have eaten a morsel. She never ate properly nor at regular hours. If Chidambaram was adamant, she would eat a little. He should have informed her before leaving.

When the ball of rice was split open, they found that the brinjal curry inside had been soaked up. They ate till their stomachs were full. Ayya scolded Chidambaram whenever he dawdled over the meal. He washed and rinsed the cloth from the food bundle. Ayya let out a small belch.

'Shall we start walking?'

'Where shall we go now?'

'Where can we go? Tell me.'

'Once we've left the village, we *have* to go somewhere.'

To the south of the irrigation tank was a big hill, with a curved peak. Around the hilltop stood a bunch of barren rock formations, like a collection of small mushrooms around a big one. Ayya was staring in the direction of the hill. It was only a short distance away.

Ayya said, 'Why don't we spend the day there?'

'Let's start, then.'

They moved away from the stream and climbed on to a rock outcrop. Cactus had grown thickly along the route. Here and there they found senna plants curled into a ball, along with thickets of coiled and intertwined jujube plants. Chidambaram cut a branch from the poolathi shrub that had grown along a ridge of hopbush. After the splinters were shaved off with the sickle, the branch could be a staff as tall as a man. The pleasant fragrance of hopbush flowers filled the air.

Ayya stopped beside a canthium plant, plucked some fruit and put them in his mouth. He also gave some to Chidambaram. When ripe, canthium fruit tasted sweet. If it was not ripe, it had to be mixed with bits of limestone and shaken vigorously in a pot to ripen it. A thirsty person found relief from chewing it. Senna fruit was different. Unless it was fully ripe, it was inedible.

Chidambaram plucked a lot of canthium fruit and put them in a pouch fashioned from a corner of his towel.

In his home town, Chidambaram enjoyed climbing the temple hill just to feast on canthium fruit. His younger sister simply loved them. She would nibble on them purposefully, like a mouse. She didn't need any other snack. Ayya brought her only boondi; sometimes he didn't even bring that for her.

'So her big brother has brought her a gift from the hill, eh?' Ayya would laugh and move on.

Chidambaram's thighs began to ache as his climb to the big hill progressed. Tired, he spat out the canthium seed in his mouth. His throat was hoarse. The sickle hanging from his waist pressed against his leg.

Ayya was climbing slowly. He didn't appear to be wearing a sickle: there was no trace of one hanging from his shoulder. He walked with his feet wide apart. He probably had a hooked blade tucked into his waist.

They heard the staccato sounds of someone chopping firewood nearby. Crested bulbuls leapt with gurgling cries among the plants and shrubs.

When he noticed Ayya turning around to look at him, he walked faster. He wanted to ask Ayya whether they really needed to climb all the way to the top. Perhaps they could stay in one of the rock caves on the hillside.

Ayya had stopped to rest in the shade.

'You look unwell. Are your legs aching? Walking barefoot here can eat up your feet.'

Chidambaram, too, halted in the shade beside his father.

'Why should they hurt? I'm used to this terrain. Aren't you barefoot yourself?'

'Are you talking about me? My feet have wandered all over, son. You are a kid born yesterday.'

As Ayya tousled his hair, the gentle breeze felt cool on his damp, sweaty skin.

'Even the midday sun doesn't sting like this. Come, let's get to the top in one go.'

'Are we staying at the top?'

'No, how can we stay there? We'll scout for a hideout down the other side. It'll be safe. Once we've checked out everything from the peak, we'll know for sure.'

When they reached the hilltop, the sun was scorching hot. The ground was not as level as it had appeared from below. The rocks stood one on top of another. A short distance away, three boulders were arranged like a shelter with one positioned like a roof over the other two. Ayya rested under its shade. Chidambaram climbed a slanted rock nearby and sat in the crook. That place was comfortable to sit in as well as convenient for scouting.

The surrounding villages and fields were as clear as in a landscape drawing. The tiny pathways seemed like lines. The ponds were like differently coloured circles, the water's colour changing with the type of soil. On the south side, however, a big hillock of similar height blocked the view.

He looked for the hill outside his home town. The temple on the hilltop was a white speck from where he sat. Rows of trees lining the road to his town looked like little saplings. Cars scurried like field mice in the gaps between the trees.

Flocks of goats began to arrive at the foothill. Cattle trudged slowly across the outcrops.

Ayya waved his hand to summon Chidambaram. He went over and sat down beside Ayya.

'The goats are here already. I'll go down on the other side and find a hideout. Keep loitering here, as if you're a goatherd.'

'Go ahead. I'll find some water to drink.'

'I am thirsty, too. I'll see if I can get some in the stream downhill.'

'I'm going to the well.'

'Are you planning to go down and climb up again?'

'Why should I climb up later? Tell me a place down below. I'll meet you there.'

Ayya paused to think.

'Yes, we should stick together, but how do we feed ourselves at noon?'

'We ate just now. Will you be hungry by noon?'

'If you're not going to be hungry, then it's all right.'

'We'll cook something for the night.'

'I am only wondering how.'

'Just give me the bag. I'll take care of the cooking.'

'I won't worry, then. Do you know how to cook?'

'It's not like climbing a hill, is it? I'll learn by doing.'

'I don't know, son. We can eat only if you cook.'

'Are you afraid I'll let you starve?'

'I won't say anything more. I'm leaving now. I'll return only after sundown. See that big tree between those two hills? Be there. I'll come there after I'm done. Keep the bag safe. Even if you put it down, don't ever keep the weapons on the ground, not even by mistake. They're our life. Even if we go hungry for a couple of days, we can still sleep peacefully. Without those weapons, we can't. I'll be off, then?'

'Give me five or six matchsticks.'

'See, I totally forgot.'

Ayya took out the matchbox from his waist pouch, took out a few sticks and gave him the box.

'Keep the box. Just a few sticks will do for me.'

Ayya got down and started walking. After a short while, he removed his shirt and wrapped it around his head. Picking up some firewood sticks, he stacked them on his head and resumed walking.

Chidambaram didn't ask Ayya where he was going. If he did, Ayya would get angry. He could ask him in the evening.

He continued watching till his father disappeared among the trees on the hillside.

His thirst had grown more acute. He had to climb

down to the foothill anyway. He had to cook, too. He had bravely reassured Ayya. Now he had to finish cooking before Ayya came back. He had no utensils. That was the big challenge. Cooking was not a big problem. He remembered how Aaththa boiled water in a pot, cleaned and dropped the rice into it, and drained the water from the rice after it was cooked. He didn't know how to make kuzhambu.

To the east, the landscape was filled with a large number of fields growing crops. He climbed down in that direction. Descending the hill was easy. He paused at regular intervals on his way down. Before crossing the stream, he placed a marker on a bush and hid the bag inside.

People were moving about in the distant fields. He entered a field planted with chillies and walked with his eyes to the ground. A cooking pot was lying inside a patch. It was a pot used for mixing and applying pesticide solution. The chemical solution had trickled over the rim. There was also a sirattai[3] inside. He collected both.

He turned and walked back to the well near the foothill. The water lay deep inside. He couldn't quench his thirst. There was no water in the kamalai pit; so he

---

[3] scoop made of one half of a coconut shell

couldn't even clean and rinse the pot. He wiped the pot with leaves, placed it upside down on his head, covered it with his towel and tied it like a mundasu. The sirattai, too, was stashed inside the mundasu. He went to the bush in which he had hidden the bag.

It took him a long time to reach the tree where he was supposed to meet his father. He walked steadily, pushing thorny plants out of the way.

He couldn't stop thinking about water. He needed a drink badly, then a little more water for cooking. If he could find water nearby, he could somehow finish cooking. Otherwise, he would have to keep on walking. Even to go to the irrigation tank, he had to make a long round trip.

Near the tree was a low-lying area. As he walked towards it, he could see green vegetation and was overjoyed. A small stream gurgled among the plants. There were two springs on one bank, their water clear.

He drank to his heart's content. Then he cleaned and scrubbed the pot with fine sand. He rinsed the sirattai too. After he had washed and rinsed the pot a few times, the chemical smell disappeared.

He assembled a stove with three stones and collected dried twigs from the area nearby. Then he gathered dried leaves from the ground and put them in the stove along with the twigs. Rubbing a part of the pot to warm it, he struck a match against it and lit a fire. He poured water in the pot and placed it on the stove to boil.

Until that moment, he hadn't thought of washing the rice and picking the stones from it before putting it in the pot. It would have been more convenient if he'd had another pot. But he would have to manage with what he had.

An idea occurred to him. There was the cloth from the food package that he had washed and dried in the morning. All he had to do was spread the cloth on the ground, put some rice on it and pick the stones from the rice. Then he could gather it in the rolled-up cloth, wash it with water and dump it straight from the cloth into the pot. He could also wrap the cloth around the neck of the pot and drain the water from the rice once it was cooked. He could use a dry twig to stir the rice. Then he had to roast a couple of dry sago chips over the fire, pulp tamarind in the sirattai and make rasam. He could transfer the cooked rice from the pot to the cloth and make rasam in the pot.

Through all these tasks, he also had to keep the bombs in the shade, away from the fire, and look out for intruders without being too distracted at the stove. There was a good chance of people passing by that way. Goats and cattle might come to the stream to drink water in the afternoon. If he managed somehow to finish cooking by then, his worries would be over for the day.

If the cooking was completed quickly, he could even explore the area near the stream. He could pluck and eat cactus fruit and taste the tang of guduchi vine. There was one species of guduchi vine that tasted sour as well as bitter. The green variety was very tasty.

~

The sun's heat had not yet subsided. He had sat in front of the fire and finished cooking their dinner. He stashed the food inside a cassia bush to protect it from dust. Then he went to the stream and washed his face. The water sparkled like porcelain. Little fishes swam and played about. Along the banks of the stream, many flowers were in bloom.

Ayya had not returned yet. Where was he? Had he gone to their village, perhaps? Why did he need to go there? They had already discussed everything in detail with Mama. He ought to be back before nightfall.

Dusk was setting in. The light on the hillside began to fade. If he crushed a little limestone powder, shaved a green stick and used it to sharpen the sickle's blade, the hours would pass by quickly. The sickle's cutting edge was blunted. Since Vadakkuraan's body was obese, the damage was limited. Else, the sickle wouldn't have withstood the impact. It would have struck a bone, and the blade would have dented.

Chopping off the arm had been as hard as cutting down a big branch from a tree. If the sickle had struck Vadakkuraan's thigh, Chidambaram would have had to strain really hard to pull it out. He wouldn't have been able to get away from there.

The blacksmith who had made the sickle was no lightweight. He was an expert in making sickles with their blades curved like a cock's tail. His skill at sharpening the blade while keeping the edge intact was truly remarkable.

The wind picked up. He cautiously explored the area, watching out for any passers-by, and settled himself on various rocks under the evening sun.

The goats and cattle that had grazed all day in the foothills were returning home to their villages. The sunlight on the rocks had receded and darkness gradually engulfed the hillside. Birds plunged swiftly into the dark and disappeared. The silence pervading the air was disrupted now and then by the roar of the wind blowing through the gorge between the hills.

After his wanderings, Chidambaram returned to the tree. He had to take each step cautiously. A stumble meant falling headlong into a bush.

He caught sight of Ayya, who was sitting with his back against a tree. Even though it couldn't have been anyone but Ayya, he stood back and watched from behind a thicket of plants.

'Come here.'

Ayya spoke in a normal voice. He had spotted Chidambaram.

'Did you come back early?'

'No. I got here just now. Where had you gone so late in the evening, son?'

'My work finished early. So I went over to the other side and looked around.'

'I saw the stove set up. I knew the job must be over.'

'I've made rice and rasam.'

'I don't *see* anything.'

Chidambaram fetched the items one by one from the cassia bush. Ayya washed his hands and came back.

'On my way back, I walked into a plantain grove and cut a couple of leaves. They're tucked inside that plant over there. Bring them.'

'We have leaves now! I was wondering how we were going to manage. Why don't you eat first? I'll eat later.'

'Sit down. We'll eat together. You've collected all these fine utensils. Smart boy.'

Spreading the banana leaves on the ground, they

served themselves rice and poured rasam over it with the sirattai. When the rice collected in the cloth was served on the plantain leaves, it smelled good. They sat behind the cover of a bush to eat, to avoid the dust from the wind.

Ayya went over to the spring to drink water and came back.

'Finish up all the rice. We don't know when we'll get to eat next. We may have to go hungry.'

'I am full already. There's some rice left. Will you have some?'

'So, you want to look after your father! Finish it. If there's rasam left, give it to me. Even your mother doesn't make rasam like this.'

After eating, Chidambaram kept the pot upside down inside the cassia bush. Ayya picked up the bag. He led Chidambaram up the hillock on the west. On their way up, Chidambaram didn't ask him about the destination; his father didn't tell him either.

A bunch of boulders lay scattered on the western outcrop. There were many types of caves formed between them. Ayya sat down in one.

'We will spend the night here, son. You lie down here. I'll head to that one over there, to the west. Can you stay alone here?'

'I'm not afraid of anything.'

'I didn't mean that. If you have no one to talk to, it might feel strange. Your weapon is your company. Keep the sickle under your head. Sleep will knock you out. Avoid keeping the bombs next to you. You might forget and turn over in your sleep.'

'I'll be safe. Go to sleep. You have run around a lot today.'

'Nothing to it. Oh, I forgot to tell you. I went looking for a place for us to stay tomorrow. It's taken me this long to come back. After tonight, we're done with this.'

'Where will we go?'

'The irrigation tank where we washed this morning.'

'It's a good spot. No one will come there.'

'No movement of cattle either. It looks secure. Once a man gets in, it will be impossible to find him. If we stay there for a day we'll find another hideout for the next day, won't we? Stopping in the same place for two or three days together is dangerous. If it's a deserted area, then we can stay.'

'Should I keep the bag here?'

'I'll keep it with me. There's a little rice left in it. Will it last us a couple of days?'

'So what if it lasts only for a day? It's nothing we can't handle.'

'We simply have to. Go and lie down.'

Ayya continued to sit unmoving, deep in thought.

'If you see someone coming, don't get up abruptly and leave. Pause for a moment and check out the surroundings before taking off. If the fellow hasn't seen you, slip out quietly and alert me by tossing a small stone. If he has, then clear your throat loudly and run away. We can meet tomorrow at the irrigation tank.'

'Who is going to come here?'

'Never think lightly of the enemy. Assume always that he is smarter than us. Not that he is smart by himself. Everything is working in his favour. The police may not come after us today. But if our enemy gives them money, they'll come running like hound dogs. So many atrocities take place in our courts. The law is what the rich people lay down.'

'We should finish off every one of those bastards.'

'Is it something you and I can do on our own? Even killing a Vadakkuraan, we had to hide and do it. That's the limit of our courage. In a sense, it's cowardly too.'

'Is it bravery only if we fight face-to-face?'

'I didn't mean that. When the enemy is strong, it takes courage even to sneak up on him. That scoundrel too destroyed people's lives by stealth. Did he have the guts to face your brother? Had he attacked your brother, the story would've been different. Your brother would have pulled out his insides and hung him at the end of a pole. The bastard had luck on his side, until yesterday. We should have put his head at your brother's feet. It still won't console us. Do you know what your mother said when she heard the fellow was dead? She was raring to go and drink his blood.'

When Ayya was angry, his voice trembled. He spoke as if he was growling. It took him a long time to calm down.

'Go to sleep.'

Ayya stood up to leave.

'If anyone attacks you head-on, don't run away. Sacrifice him to the hill.'

The stink of animal droppings in the cave was stronger now. Chidambaram plucked a few blades of stylo grass from a corner and took a sniff. Its ginger smell masked the odour of animal droppings.

He spread the towel and lay down on it with his head inside the cave. He kept the sickle and the bombs next to his head on the right. A few pebbles pressed into his back. He put his hand under the towel and removed them.

Ayya wouldn't have slept by now. His face darkened with grief whenever he thought of Annan. He drank arrack every day to forget. He talked a lot only when he was drunk.

Four or five days ago, drunk on arrack, Ayya had called Mama well before nightfall to accompany him to Vadakkur.

Mama rebuked Ayya and calmed him down.

'Don't talk as if you're a little child, machaan. There's a time for everything. No need to shoot your mouth off.'

Ayya lay on the floor, grumbling to himself. Mama remained sitting, without saying anything.

This had happened many times. Ayya would get low like this. Sometimes he broke down and cried.

Even during the daytime, if Ayya happened to think about Annan, he would leave the house. When they looked for him, they would find him lying on his side under the black babul tree, raised head resting on a palm. Or he would be sitting quietly, playing with his sickle in the dirt. Chidambaram would have to bring him home for his midday meal.

After his brother died, no one in Chidambaram's house had been able to sleep properly.

Field mice screeched. Bats collided into stone. Partridges groaned in the cactus shrubs. Behind the bushes, a rabbit's scream rose and died. Collecting his weapons, he walked over to that side. A vulture flew into the dark, making an ugly sound with its flapping wings. At the mouth of a burrow, a rabbit lay mauled. The vulture had plucked out its eyes and liver. After removing the intestines, he wrapped the rest in a bunch of leaves.

On the way back, he saw a barn owl sitting on a rock, staring with its round eyes wide open. It didn't move until he was very close. He was about to throw a bomb at it, but stopped himself. He picked up a stone instead and threw it at the bird. It flew away with an ugly hoot.

Once he was back in the rock hole, he stowed the rabbit meat in a shelf high above and lay down to sleep.

Ayya had had such stature and bearing once. Everything in him had shrivelled up. Now he was shy of wielding a weapon.

There was no weapon he hadn't handled back in the day. They had every kind at home, not just a few. He would always keep at least four or five types: poleaxe, dagger, armlet, springblade, and a serrated knife shaped like a cock's tail – he owned all these and more. If he carried a round stick, it would have a knife hidden inside. Mama would tease him. 'What, machaan, are you off to pull out weeds with that weeding hook of yours?'

'Yes, to remove weeds. If you don't get rid of them, they won't let the crop grow.'

'You are like a little boy with his toy.'

'Maapillai, you're making fun of me, but have you ever seen the entrance to the police station?'

'I have, too. What about it?'

'Do you think there are heaps of gold in there? Even so, every policeman is allowed to keep a weapon tucked behind his arse and one more in front, along with a round club in his hand. But *we* are not allowed to carry weapons. Those lifeless wimps are asked to carry a rifle one day and a club the next. But if *we* do the same thing, it's a crime. I feel pity when I see them; I also feel angry. It's not as if everyone is constantly rebelling against them.'

'That's their duty.'

'This is my duty, then.'

'Go ahead. Have it your way.'

During the cropping season, Chidambaram slept many nights in the field along with Ayya. He loved it.

Ayya told them plenty of old stories. He would narrate everything as if it happened yesterday. He would go on late into the night till sleep engulfed them.

~

Annan was with them back then.

The sorghum crop in their land was ripe for harvesting. The seed company's white sorghum variety had produced a bumper crop. Vadakkuraan, too, had planted sorghum in all his lands. Seen from a distance, the area looked like one big grove.

Along with Annan and Chidambaram, Ayya was standing guard in the eastern corner of the field. They had brought a pot of coffee and palm sugar with them. Ayya carried the only flashlight.

Chidambaram felt a craving for corn. He asked his brother, 'Shall we boil some corn with palm sugar?'

'Ask Ayya.'

Ayya didn't say no.

'If one of you can go home and bring palm sugar for our coffee, I have no problem,' he said.

Annan suggested gently: 'Let Chidambaram cook the corn. I'll go home and come back.'

Annan took the flashlight from Ayya and set out. Chidambaram went to pick and strip a bunch of tender corn ears.

Ayya called out from the corner, 'Do a check all around the field.'

As he was walking along the north side, a ball of mud thrown from the middle of the field fell at his feet. Ignoring it, he surveyed all four sides and went back. His father asked him casually, 'What was it? I heard a rustling noise.'

Chidambaram was unfazed.

'Somebody pelted a mud ball. I also thought of tossing a few in that direction. But it was our own man, so I kept quiet.'

Ayya laughed without moving his head.

'Our lad is quite brave, it seems. I don't have to come here on guard duty any more. I can huddle at home and protect myself from the cold.'

'Did you wonder whether I could guard this field alone?'

'I only want a son who can.'

Ayya went his own way, always, in all matters. Ayya once overheard Chidambaram asking his mother for a water-gourd shell that he could use to learn swimming. He bit his lip in anger.

'So you want a water-gourd shell? Come, I'll give it to you.'

Ayya took him to the well and dropped him into it. Chidambaram was terrified. He swallowed a lot of water at first, but when he finally managed to kick with his feet, Ayya swam over, held him steady with a palm under his belly and gently taught him how to swim.

After three days of bathing in the well with Ayya, his inhibitions vanished. By the fourth day, he had learnt to swim.

One day, Ayya brought a water-gourd shell from the field, gave it to him and asked him to bathe in the well.

He was scared to go bathing with Ayya. Ayya would hold him with one hand and bathe him. Sometimes he made Chidambaram sit on his lap and scrubbed him hard. Whenever Chidambaram had an oil bath, Ayya banged hard on his skull to push the oil into the scalp. His head felt sore for the next four days. Finally, Aaththa told Ayya, 'You're going to crush our growing boy to the floor by pounding his head.'

'No need of false growth for him. Even if a rock falls on his head, he should brush it off and carry on.' Ayya banged even harder on Chidambaram's head.

By the time Annan came back, the corn was ready, and they mixed it with palm sugar. After the three of them finished eating it, they prepared and drank coffee. Ayya stretched out in the now empty main water channel while his two sons lay down in two branch channels.

The rustle of swaying corn stalks filled the field.

'Has Chidambaram dozed off? Is this how you guard the field?' Ayya asked, raising his head to look.

He shot back immediately, 'I thought I heard you snoring.'

Annan tittered. Ayya sighed.

'Do you think I slept properly when I was young?'

'Why?'

'We slept in the fields half the time, along with our families.'

'Why couldn't you sleep at home, then?'

'We were scared that the villagers might come any time and set fire to the house. The women and children slept inside; my father and I had to stand outside all night and guard the house.'

'Was there so much hatred against you?'

'We had a lot of enemies. The rich men would get together and rouse others in the village against us.'

Annan was angry.

'Why would anyone want to live like that? You should have killed every one of them, laid them face up on the ground and walked away.'

'A man can't survive on rage alone, son. They would deliberately raise havoc in his land. If he protested there'd be trouble.'

Chidambaram said testily, 'You should've let it come.'

'Most of the villagers were with him. We had no one on our side. People were afraid of losing their livelihood. What could we do? We suffered alone. When my father drew water from the well, a sickle was hanging from the frame of the water lift. When I watered the fields, a sickle was hanging from a castor plant.'

'How many days did you spend like that?'

'Not just one or two days. This went on from when I was a child till I grew up.'

'Why did they torment you like that?'

'No reason. The rich guys couldn't stomach the fact that we were farming our own piece of land. They wanted us to give it up and go away.'

'Was it their ancestral property?'

'No, but they had grabbed properties from a lot of people.'

'Should you have let them get away with it?'

'I also thought about it every single day. The way it went on, I thought I wouldn't be able to live normally with women. So I decided to resolve it one way or the other.'

Ayya fell silent. Annan was furious.

'So you had to think a lot before deciding, eh?'

'Had I been alone, I wouldn't have. How could I abandon my mother, sister and father? My family would have been wiped out.'

'That's true.'

'So we hatched a plan. Four days before the strike, we drove our two bulls to my uncle's village. It was ten miles away to the east. We told the women to collect their household items and go there. We asked our supporters in the village to be alert that night. No need for anyone to come with us, we told them. I picked up a spear staff. My father carried a sickle. The barnyard next to one fellow's mortar house had a thatched roof. I sneaked behind the house and set fire to it. Ayya pelted stones into the village. People woke up and there was utter confusion. The fellow came out of the mortar house through the back door. Hiding near the wall, I got him with one stab in the belly. We sprinted back and set our own house on fire. There was a big crowd. Even after we'd run very far, we could still hear the commotion in the village. Light from the blaze was visible on the horizon like a giant burning torch. I never stepped near my native village again . . . Did you bring the bidi bundle, son?'

Annan handed it to Ayya.

'What did Aththai and Paati do later?'

'They worked as coolies to survive. Your periya thaatha took them into his family. We sold everything we owned and fought the case. They gave both of us nine years each. Thaatha was acquitted in the appellate court. My sentence was upheld.'

'How did they let him off?'

'Thaatha had gone away to some other village at

sunset that day and returned only the next day. So it was proved that he wasn't present in the village at the time of the murder. A good man from that village gave evidence.'

'So you went off to jail, then?'

'I went away to the city. Your grandfather went back to the village with his brother.'

'You came here straight from prison?'

'I had to make a living. Going back to the western fields would have meant more trouble. My family had already moved from there. So I took off alone. When I got here, I was young and strong. I took up all kinds of work: broke stones in a quarry, worked as a mason's helper, joined an eatery and did cart trips all day, fetching water from the local pond. I left that too and finally worked as a farmhand in your uncle's household for a monthly wage. It was then that I became fond of your mother. But that's an old story … others in your uncle's family didn't like it. But he was adamant and saw our marriage through. He built us a separate house. Even this land that we are sleeping on right now was gifted by him in your mother's name.'

Chidambaram was curious.

'What happened to the land in your village?'

'It's lying fallow.'

'We should farm it.'

'We'll definitely farm it some day, sooner or later.'

'Hunh.' Ayya sighed. Annan asked him, 'Didn't Mama say anything?'

'If we'd gone by his wish, we'd be living there now. He had second thoughts, though. We had two children by then. He saw your mother's situation and said, "Stay here with us."'

'Company for Aththai, too.'

'Aththai is a quiet soul. I was the one who approached her family and got her married to Mama. At first, Mama had wanted to marry a woman from my village. I was not in favour. It would have led to unnecessary trouble. "Drop the idea, maapillai," I told him. Today, he has fathered a daughter. A son will bring confidence to that woman.'

'Have you visited Thaatha and Paati in their village recently?'

'Thaatha passed away many years ago. I didn't go to cremate him. They didn't send word to me. They feared that I would turn up there if they told me. So I couldn't see my father's face before he was cremated. What could I do, going later? I had the ritual dip right here. Mama bought me a dhoti and towel. It's four or five years since I saw Paati. I've asked her to come here for visaakam festival. Your aunts, too, got married over there. Periyappa made all the arrangements like they were his own family. And we are stuck here like this.'

Chidambaram felt like yawning. Annan had already become quiet.

Mama was a smart man. He was very fond of Aaththa. He never failed to consult her in any matter that came up in his household. 'Emma, Sundari, what do you think about this?' he would ask her often. If he had to buy a piece of land or property, he would visit their home the previous day and give her the amount he had to pay for it. He would come the next morning, enter the house without touching the door frame, fold his palms together and collect the money from his sister.

Mama's family owned fields and groves adjacent to the village. They had bullock carts and pump sets. Even though there were servants at home to do the work, Mama would run around everywhere himself. If Aththai went to the field, Aaththa would go with her. Aaththa had to attend to everything. While planting seedlings, she had to step into the land and hand them out for planting. Similarly, while harvesting corn ears, she had to ceremonially cut the first one. Mama would invite her home during the harvest season and give her more than enough grain for her family's needs.

Ayya was of great help to Mama in everything

he did. They treated each other with warmth and mutual respect. They routinely exchanged confidences. When they were both drunk it was quite a sight. They practically embraced and rolled around while talking to each other. If he had drunk a bit too much, Ayya would weep and moan. His speech would become embarrassing and unpleasant. Mama was not like that. Even if he had drunk a whole pot of arrack, he would never show it. He would talk without losing his composure.

No one could control Ayya when he was drunk. He would brazenly raise his hand against anyone in front of him. Aaththa and Aththai would wail loudly and complain to Mama. Mama put up with Ayya's behaviour only up to a point. If he couldn't take it any more, he would end it with no more than a couple of phrases.

'Machaan, will you go inside the house and sleep, or should I force you to lie down?'

That was it. Ayya wouldn't say a word. All his antics would cease in no time.

All three of them began to fall asleep in the sorghum field.

It must have been midnight. They heard rustling noises in another corner of the field. A few coughs. Regular tapping sounds: 'chadak, chadak'. Annan woke up. He nudged Ayya. Still prone, Ayya signalled back to him. As the sounds came closer and closer, Annan started to get up. Ayya caught his hand and made him sit down. Then he called out, 'Brother Muthaiah! There is a bit of our land here. Watch it.'

A voice came from the other side. 'Why, brother? How could we steal from your children? Is that why you've come to stand guard?'

The rustling noise receded into the distance. Only the taps – chadak, chadak – could be heard clearly.

Ayya said, laughing, 'Listen to the noise those cracked soles are making with the sandals.'

Annan was amazed.

'They might be stealing, but they seem to have a rule about where they can steal from!'

'They are highly disciplined. They won't enter the fields of hard-working people.'

'Why should they roam around all night, stealing from others? Why can't they work to earn a living?'

Annan lay down again.

'They did all kinds of farming once. They were quite well off, too. A couple of rich landlords in the village didn't like it. One of them was Vadakkuraan. The two brothers were united, but he goaded them to fight with each other and watched the fun. The fight eventually led to murder and more deaths. The fellows on both sides carried their food bundles and trudged regularly to the courts to fight the case. They sold off all their lands to pay off third parties, ending up finally in this situation.'

'Shouldn't they have a bit of sense at least? It's not like they *had* to behave recklessly and ruin themselves.'

'It looks that way to a third party. If you give in to your anger, you'll forget everything. You realize it only when your head hits the doorstep. Take me. I had to leave my village, didn't I?'

'Well, you finished off a rich landlord.'

'These fellows clashed with their own family members. It was convenient for Vadakkuraan. He took over their lands.'

'Shouldn't they have figured it out?'

'They didn't know in the beginning. The arrogance of money had made them blind.'

'Are they together now at least?'

'Yes, they are very united when they steal.'

'Can't they do any other work?'

'Who will hire them? Vadakkuraan has built a farmstead with all the land he has grabbed. He has hired permanent farmhands on monthly wages. He is not going to call these two men for any work. So they've decided that this is the only alternative. They steal all night and sleep during the day.'

'What'll they do if they get caught?'

'No one says they are evil. They don't steal too much, just enough to feed their families. If they need spending money, they pick cotton.'

'At night?'

'The cotton bolls are clearly visible when there's moonlight. They pick them and put them in a sack, carry it to an open area and strip the cotton from the bolls. They know all about who is growing what in the punjai[4] lands of all the surrounding villages. They will never step inside land that belongs to a poor man. This Muthaiah, he even comes to mediate cases.'

'Really?'

'He mediates in all kinds of disputes. A funny thing happened once. I had gone to watch a hearing. Mama hadn't come. Muthaiah was present. He was smartly turned out in a brand-new dhoti. Where did you buy this, I asked him. He said the dhoti had grown in a cotton plantation. I discovered his secret only later. Just like his gang, another gang had come to the same field to steal cotton one night. Both gangs met at some point. Armed with a stick in his hand, Muthaiah hid himself in a corner. That gang was foraging in the

---

[4] rain-fed land where dryland crops like millets and cotton are grown

55

punjai land of an innocent farmer. Muthaiah didn't like it. From behind a mulberry tree, he threw stones at them and they ran away. A gang member who was lagging behind tripped and his dhoti came loose. He left it there and ran away. Our Muthaiah picked it up, wore it and walked out.'

'Do these gangs enter into fights?'

'They never fight. Muthaiah was angry because that gang had entered a field they shouldn't have. That day, during the hearing, Muthaiah and the man who lost his dhoti met alone and had a private talk. After Muthaiah scolded him, they both went into the village and came back. Muthaiah had returned the new dhoti and came back wearing an old one. When they left, Muthaiah promised to return the old dhoti in a couple of days.'

'He is a good man.'

'Despite everything that's happened to him he won't touch a drop of liquor. Even when all sorts of people tried to take him along and trip him up, it was impossible. So clever he was. One day, they'd gone to steal corn ears. Muthaiah was checking out one side while the others were roaming around on the other side. The watchmen were also asleep on the other side. As soon as they saw the watchmen, the gang of thieves dispersed.'

'Leaving Muthaiah behind?'

'Nobody noticed him. The guards were lying in two different corners of the field. Hearing the noise, one of them woke up and shone his flashlight. Muthaiah didn't know what to do. He couldn't run away. With the corns on his feet, he couldn't take even a single step without his flip-flops. It would've done him no good to stand there, in an unfamiliar place, and try to handle the situation.'

'Caught red-handed, eh?'

'By this time, the guards' conversation was audible. Muthaiah racked his brain. He listened keenly to their talk. They were speaking in Telugu. He got his courage back. He slipped away to the nearest corner and struck the wet channel with his stick. Then, the sound of someone wailing in Telugu, "Oh mother, I am dying," was heard.'

'Who was that?'

'Our Muthaiah himself. The sequence continued: a blow, followed by a wail. The guards didn't linger; they took off towards the village. Muthaiah walked away casually from there. As soon as he got back to his village, he gave the others a severe scolding.'

'It was only right. How could they ditch him in some remote field?'

'This is how they make their living now. If everyone

had their own piece of land, why would they go through all this trouble? They would work quietly on their own land, wouldn't they? Whenever I think about that, I want to hold on to our land in spite of all the hardships we may face. Otherwise, given all that Vadakkuraan is tempting us with, this land would have gone into his hands long ago.'

Sleep overpowered them at sunrise.

~

By the time he fell asleep in the rock hole on the barren outcrop, the day was beginning to dawn. He got up, flapped his dhoti vigorously and wore it. He packed the utensils and retrieved the rabbit meat.

Chidambaram must wake Ayya without waiting for him to get up and come over. He must be careful not to touch Ayya, who might simply grab his weapon and pounce.

Aaththa was alert in such matters. She would stand close to Ayya and call Annan's name. Ayya would wake up instantly on hearing her call even if he was in deep slumber.

Chidambaram went to the cave where Ayya was sleeping and tossed a stone at him.

'Ah, you've come early. I thought I would come over after some time.'

'It's daybreak now. Let's go away before people can recognize our faces.'

They started out in the darkness before dawn.

3

'Is it Wednesday already? By now they must have finished cutting up his corpse. Once that's over, they will file a case. The police will line up witnesses to give evidence in court.'

Ayya was uprooting plants and dead vegetation from a patch inside the irrigation tank.

'Must have been like laying a buffalo on its side and hacking it.'

'Yes, he was a beefy fellow.'

'When his hand fell on my foot, it felt so heavy.'

'If the fingers clutch on to something at that point, it can't be pulled out.'

'I thought of bringing the hand with me, but it was too heavy. I didn't want it; so I kicked it out of the way and took off.'

'Bring it and make soup, eh?'

Ayya threw away a thorny branch.

Wielding a plant like a broom, Chidambaram levelled the patch.

'Who will come forward to give evidence?'

'The police will find them somewhere. There are so many wretches waiting to swear an oath in court for five or ten rupees … but I don't think anyone will come forward in this fellow's case.'

'They must have definitely put down the shopkeeper as a witness. He had seen me earlier that evening. I had bought snacks for Thangachi in his shop. I buy there regularly.'

'He is a harmless fellow. I don't think he will testify.'

'Who else, then?'

'That rogue who is the supervisor in Vadakkuraan's house? He is sure to testify. He was Vadakkuraan's henchman.'

'Arrogant bastard! He'll turn up in court. I should have stabbed him first.'

'If he testifies, he'll be slaughtered next. Anything that happens next is all right by me. But I don't think he will play mischief now that his master is done for.'

'It would be wise of him to feel scared.'

'He is such a haughty fellow. It won't be easy for him.'

'Who will pay the price, then? Anyway, let things

happen as they will. Will they name you as the first accused in the case? Are they such idiots?'

'Do you think they'll add you?'

'Definitely.'

'I'll confess that I did it. What will they do then?'

'They may not believe you. You're not even fifteen, so how would you have the guts to do it alone? They'll say I was the one who pushed you to do it. Or they'll cook up a story that I'd done it and asked you to confess.'

'Will they add Mama too?'

'We'll see how it plays out. We'll know when we meet him.'

They had trimmed the patch to look like a miniature threshing floor. It was a convenient place to sit, hidden from view by a dense growth of babul trees.

They could observe people moving about on the embankment. Its location was such that they could conveniently escape from the back by running along the ridge to the hill or swimming to the bank. The place was cool, too, being close to a waterbody. Ayya had cleared the patch so neatly that Chidambaram felt like lying down to sleep immediately.

Ayya walked over to another spot and started clearing it. They had decided that they should sleep separately, just as they had done on the hill.

'While you are busy clearing, I'll go across to the bank and find a pot for us. We have to cook something for lunch.'

'We *have* to do it, eh? How a man has to struggle for the sake of his eight-inch belly! Why can't we stop feeling hungry? It would be great if we need to eat only once in ten days. All right, then. Go ahead. Move carefully with your weapons. Take the longer path.'

Chidambaram walked away, deep in thought. After circling the spillage channel, he climbed the sluice and surveyed the scene. The area north of the embankment was an expanse of agricultural fields. In most of them, there was a luxuriant growth of groundnut plants. Women were working in a few fields. Most of these had a plantain grove or a betel garden.

Once he was past the sluice gate, he climbed down the outer slope and walked along the main channel.

He heard rustling sounds near a thorn bush. Two men were shaking the bush with long poles. A third man held a stick with a trident fixed at one end, in readiness to strike. What were they hunting?

Suddenly a big snake slithered out. The man holding the trident stabbed it in the head. Unable to move, it swung its tail and twirled itself around the stick. The men's faces lit up with joy.

One man gripped the snake's head and rolled its

body around his arm. With its head in a tight grip, the snake rolled its tongue out like a string and drew it back. He stroked the snake's body from neck to tail, removing the dirt on its skin. The snake's body swelled like a blower and then subsided. It was a long, slimy Indian ratsnake.

The second took a knife out from its cloth wrapping and neatly cut off the snake's head. Then, holding it stretched on the ground, he cut the snake from head to tail, deftly peeling away the skin and rolling it up like a hand-drum. He fastened it with the tail-end and dropped it into his bag. Stripped of its skin, the snake was a quivering mess of flesh and blood.

Soon another man from the hunting party picked up the dirt from a burrow and smelled it. He gave it to the other two to smell. All three nodded and began to dig into the burrow with sticks. One of them put his hand inside the hole and tugged the snake by its tail, but he was unable to pull it out.

They started digging now in earnest. Eventually one of them managed to grip the snake's tail, slide his hand down its body and hold it just below the head. Then he stabbed it in the head and pulled it out. It was a cobra. They peeled off its skin too. After plucking a tick from the skin, they rolled it up. Then they left the area.

Chidambaram was amazed that they knew exactly where to hunt. They seemed to have no fear of snakes and were highly disciplined: until they had finished hunting both the snakes, no one had uttered a word. Such focus and courage was rare. The accuracy with which the men had killed the snakes was incredible.

Chidambaram entered a cluster of palm trees. Pots to collect padaneer were hung on them. He removed his shirt, leaving the sickle hanging from his waist, and hid it. Then he started to climb a tree with many pots. As he went higher, the palm tree grew thicker. He stopped midway and stretched his legs. When he climbed to the top and gripped the stalk, he was reminded of snakes.

Snakes climbed up palm trees to catch the flies swarming over the padaneer pots. They would be nestling comfortably in the grooves.

He crouched over a palm stalk and looked into the pots. Since the morning's yield had been taken down, very little padaneer had collected in the pots. He untied two pots and transferred their contents to the others. He also shifted the flat leaves that had been squeezed into them to other pots without letting them drip. Fastening the empty pots to his waist string, he saw a big pot tied behind a dripping stalk. It was the only one which had not been coated with lime.

'What a messy way to tap toddy!'

He climbed down, chuckling to himself.

When he reached the irrigation tank, he couldn't see Ayya. Then he heard his father's groaning. He looked up. High above, his father had trimmed a few babul branches and arranged the forked branches into a hammock. He was lying comfortably in it.

'So, you've collected a couple of cooking pots? You seem to get them as if on order.'

'I stole a couple of padaneer pots.'

'Did you climb a palm tree, you crazy boy? There is no better way to give yourself away. If a toddy tapper catches you, you'll be done for.'

'No one was around. I climbed up only after checking.'

'They must be tapping toddy along with padaneer.'

'They've hung a big pot. Go and help yourself.'

Ayya's face grew dark. He didn't say anything. He climbed down slowly. Chidambaram set off with the pots to fetch water.

Ayya started to cut the rabbit meat. Seeing the sickle in action, Chidambaram lit the fire.

'It's a lot of meat for two people. If you let the meat stink and then roast it over a fire, it will taste delicious.'

'You'll want something along with the meat, won't you?'

Ayya looked up. His face betrayed no emotion.

'You're still a young lad. What do you know about that? If there is liquor to go with so much meat, it'd be really special.'

'How will you forget the taste, even after all this . . .?'

'After all what . . .? Have you ever seen me doing something wrong? Do I beg anyone for liquor?'

Ayya threw his bidi away and stood up.

'That you never do. But it's always the other fellow who supplies liquor to you.'

'So?'

'Nothing. Just be quiet. I'll go over to the other side and collect firewood. Keep an eye on the pot.'

Chidambaram entered the thicket. While he was walking inside, he thought about Ayya. He needn't have spoken so harshly. The things that Mama had told him! Ayya couldn't control his drinking. The thicket of vines inside the tank was really dense. In several places, he couldn't take a step forward. Little birds that he had never seen before were flitting about. Crested birds, birds with fantails, birds with hair covering their feet – there were so many varieties. The clearing was filled with their chatter.

Water willow covered the ground. Resin had seeped out of the babul trees. He climbed up the trees and cut the resin deposit of the trunks.

Honeybees were descending on a senna plant. When he went closer, he found a large beehive. He pulled out a blade of elephant grass and gently poked the part full of honey without disturbing the bees. It was dripping with honey. If he had a pole arm, he could pull the hive close, then chew a nettle plant and blow on it.

He took his shirt off and covered his face with it. Then he spat a couple of times on the honeycomb and shook the senna plant. The bees dispersed and flew upward, spinning together giddily like a tangled ball of jute string.

He held down the branch with the honeycomb and tore off the brood comb with the larvae on it. Only the honey pot was now left sticking to the branch. Even so, a couple of bees stung his arm. He pulled out the broken stingers from his skin.

If only Muthamma Paati, his grandmother, were alive now. She loved to eat the brood comb, tearing it into bits and chewing it like a sweet. Juice from the crushed larvae would dribble from the corners of her mouth. Eating larvae sharpened one's eyesight, apparently. She even earned the nickname of 'honeycomb hag'.

Annan was very fond of her. Whenever he happened to pick a honeycomb while grazing goats, he would save the brood comb and give it to her. She would bless him generously when he brought her some: 'May all my grandchildren live long and prosper.'

Annan was an expert in extracting honey. No matter how high the tree, he would climb up and capture the hive. He wasn't afraid of even mountain bees, entering rock holes to gather their honey. The very buzz of the mountain bee was scary. Whee, whee . . . it pursued a man relentlessly.

Once, when Annan was gathering honey from a hole inside the sheath of a well, the bees chased him and he had to drop into the well. He was able to float some broken pieces of dung cakes on the water, making the bees sit on them, and escape from a corner.

Even then, he did not give up on the bounty. Two days later, he returned with a burning torch and captured the hive.

If people needed honey for medical use, the neighbours would ask Annan. There would always be a full bottle of honey hanging on the wall. If a goat or draught animal chewed on a toxic plant and fell unconscious, honey was a good antidote. Apart from honey, there would always be a stock of dry pongam pods in the house, and porcupine skin as well. People would come running to Annan when their babies contracted whooping cough. There was no one else who would thoughtfully collect and keep medicinal items the way Annan did. He was always prepared.

~

Crow pheasants hopped and ran between the trees on the tank bed. They didn't fly most of the time. With such large wings, the wretched birds could go quite far, but they would only loiter about like lazy donkeys.

Some days, Chidambaram would set the dog on them. Even then, they would only run to escape. If exhausted, they would take cover behind a thicket of thorn trees. Having caught their scent, the dog would wag its tail and leap about.

He wished his dog was with him now. He wondered how it was staying confined to the house. If it gave them a lot of trouble, they would tie it up. It would growl constantly as if it was cursing someone. The dog was definitely an extra burden for Aththai.

Mama must be hiding somewhere outside the village. What would happen if they added Mama to the list of accused in the case, as Ayya predicted? It was quite likely. There were many people around who bore a grudge against him.

Mama was street-smart. He handled every issue

with discernment. Otherwise, he would have gone to jail several times by now.

Chidambaram felt an urge to meet his uncle. Mama would talk to him as if to an adult. He would talk to him about so many things, from how to sharpen a knife on a stone slab to how to carry one's weapons hidden without letting them show. He was a man who could walk normally even while carrying a hatchet close to his ribs.

Chidambaram must talk to Ayya about meeting Mama. If they kept on like this, the days would slip away. If Ayya agreed, he could go to the village, meet Mama and come back. If Mama was not in the village, he could ask Mama's friend Ayyanar. Mama would never go anywhere without informing Ayyanar.

Aththai would be all alone. She wouldn't have anyone to talk to. Aaththa, too, would be away. Aththai didn't have Aaththa's strength of spirit. If she was hurt, she would sigh and close her eyes. Like pearls of sorghum, tears would spill and flow from her eyes. He wanted to meet and comfort her.

He had seen her tear-filled face on the day they left. She didn't have a life as happy as she deserved.

He wondered about their house. The police would have certainly broken the door frame at the entrance. If anyone provoked them, they could go wild. The police would have harassed their neighbours too. For the death of one man, why should everyone in their village get thrashed?

That was a peculiar trait of policemen. If they were real men, they should catch the criminal. It would prove that they were capable men. Harassing women and children seemed cowardly.

Many such incidents had happened in their town. Someone would have committed a crime, and the police would haul some blameless man to the police station. They would keep him there for two days without food or drink. Sometimes they would name a man who had done nothing as an accused in the case.

Was it right to keep a man in chains, like a dog? They took pleasure in taking in a healthy, strong man, battering his whole body and sending him back. No one could challenge them. Their word was law.

When he stopped to think about the last few days, he felt that they shouldn't have run away. As soon as he cut down Vadakkuraan, he should have walked into the police station. He had run away only because he wanted to seek Mama's advice.

Ayya never talked about it. If Chidambaram broached the topic, he would get angry. He had to ask him today somehow.

In one hand he held a stack of firewood. In

his other hand he carried a lump of resin and the honeycomb. He turned to Ayya, who was returning from the stream with a pot full of water.

'You seem to have a lot of things in your hands.'

'I found resin on the trees and collected some. On my way back, I even found a honeycomb.'

He held out the honeycomb. Ayya took it, broke off a piece and put it in his mouth. His face lit up with pleasure.

In the evening, the calm of the tank bed was disrupted. After the day's work in the fields, people walked along the embankment, chatting among themselves. Someone closed the sluice gate and walked on.

They sat on the embankment and chatted till sunset. He listened with rapt attention to his father while enjoying the sight of the fish jumping in the water.

Since they had free time in the evening, they finished eating the leftover rice from the afternoon. Ayya didn't want to eat so early. He had said that he would prefer to eat after it was dark. But Chidambaram forced him. He had to tie the pots back on the palm tree, didn't he, before the traffic of people started?

Ayya was a bit hurt.

'You go out as you please and wander where you like. What shall we do if something happens to you?'

'Who will come here, anyway?'

'It's not right to talk like that. This village nearby, do you know anything about it?'

'I've never been there.'

'Many of Vadakkuraan's relations live there. By chance, if one of them spots you . . . why go out of your way to invite trouble?'

'If trouble wants to come after us, let it come.'

'We can talk like this when we are in our own place, son. It's easy for *you* to talk. If something happened to you, how would I answer to anybody? How could I face your uncle after that? How could I bear to tell your mother? Your aunt would die of grief.' Ayya's voice became hoarse.

'What's happened now to make you say such things? I won't go out any more.'

Ayya said after a while, 'We are out of rice. What shall we do tomorrow?'

He thought about it for a moment.

'We have to manage somehow.'

'How?'

'I'll sell the resin and buy some rice.'

'Should I eat what you provide for? I told you clearly just a short while ago. And you're saying this now.'

'Will you go out and buy food, then?'

'Let's go hungry tomorrow.'

Ayya looked at him. The boy said confidently: 'Only the destitute have to go without food. We have the money. Why should we starve?'

'All right, son. Let's say I don't have the means.'

'I'll buy it then. I'll go to our village, meet Mama and get everything we need.'

'Just say you want to see Mama.'

'Yes.'

'If he'd given us enough rice to last for a long time, we could have met him later, right?'

'If he'd given us a whole sack, we could eat and roam around happily. But he is not so thoughtless as to make us carry a heavy load, is he? Are we going to seek him out now only to ask for rice?'

'What else should we meet him for?'

'And don't we have to meet him and find out what's going on?'

'What will you do after finding out?'

'You'll say that, won't you? If I'd gone straight to the station that day, we wouldn't be in this trouble. All of you are suffering because of me . . .'

Ayya patted his back.

'Even if you had surrendered, do you think we can stay put? The trouble starts only now. The police will harass everyone. Would anyone with any sense charge a minor as the first accused in a murder case?'

Chidambaram asked after a brief interval of silence, 'Then, don't we have to meet Mama?'

'We have to, yes.'

'Staying here?'

'He'll come tomorrow.'

'How do you know that?'

'I met him yesterday.'

'You said you were going to the tank.'

'How can I spend the whole day looking at a small tank? I went straight to the village and got all the news.'

'Was Mama at home?'

'How do you expect him to be home? But I managed to locate him. He is buzzing about the town.'

'Didn't you see Aththai?'

'I did. She carries food to Mama every day.'

He was happy to hear that. He didn't ask any more probing questions. When Mama comes tomorrow, I can get all the news from him, he thought.

He hadn't suspected that Ayya might have gone to the village. Ayya could have told him of his plan while they were chatting. But Ayya kept many things to himself.

Spending the night inside the tank was a new experience. Because of the constant lapping of water in the tank, he could not sleep undisturbed. Exhausted from his outings the previous day, Ayya went quietly to sleep.

Peace in their family had been eroded with every passing year, and now it had left them stranded in this irrigation tank. When the visaakam festival came around, it would be a day of mourning and tears for his mother and aunt. Had their house ever been so sad during visaakam?

~

Janaki was alive then.

Everyone in their family had bought new clothes for visaakam that year. Aaththa had bathed early in the morning and worn her new sari.

She had inserted small wreaths of davana buds in her hair and thali[5] string. As she bent forward, her braided hair fell like a mat over her ears.

Seeing her husband and elder son together, Aaththa said, 'You look like brothers already. After a

[5] sacred string/chain worn around the neck by women as a sign of marital bond/status

few years, no one will be able to tell father and son apart.'

Chidambaram was sitting on the pyol,[6] fondling his new clothes. He had not bathed yet. Ayya shouted at him: 'Elei, Chelambaram. Why are you sitting in a corner without putting on your new shirt?'

Chidambaram was silent, evidently in a sulk. His mother muttered as she passed by, 'This little child wants me to bathe him, I think.'

Aththai's voice was heard at the entrance. 'Why is Chelambaram looking out of sorts today?'

His mother looked at him mischievously. 'You have to ask your son-in-law and find out.'

Putting an arm around his shoulder, Aththai led him away. 'Keep this new shirt here and come home. You can wear it tomorrow.'

As they were leaving, Aaththa mumbled, 'Why won't he sulk if he is pampered so much?'

Aththai bathed him, made him wear the shirt that Mama had bought for him and enjoyed his fine appearance.

Dressed in her new clothes, Janaki sat on the doorstep, nibbling a snack. She was watching them.

---

[6] waist-high stone or cement platform that usually flanks the entrance to a traditional house, outside the main doorway

Aththai smiled at her. 'Chelambaram has come, finally. Shall we all eat together?'

Mama's voice came from inside the house: 'Janaki is going to serve food to everyone today.'

Ayya had come over, looking for him. He asked Mama, 'Maapillai, why are you trying to entice Chelambaram so early?'

Mama didn't give an inch. 'Do I have to lure a boy for my daughter? Do you think he won't come to her doorstep and wait around like a dog?'

'We'll see about that.'

'What's there to see? Can't you see the young rake hanging about?'

Ayya scowled at Chidambaram. 'Elei, look at your uncle bragging. If you come here again, I'll skin your hide,' Ayya mocked his son. Chidambaram ran to his uncle and held on to his hand.

Janaki was no longer at the doorstep. She hid herself whenever she saw Ayya. Ayya looked at Aththai. 'I can't see my elder mother-in-law. Where is she? I've come specially to eat from her hand.'

Aththai went to Janaki, who was standing inside next to a mound of grain. 'Mama has come here asking for food. Ask him to have lunch with us, or he'll be angry with you.'

Ayya called out from the pyol, 'I don't want food, 'ma. Just show me your face; it will fill my belly.'

Janaki peeped out from behind Aththai.

'What a sight. That's enough, 'ma. My stomach is completely full. I'll take leave now.'

He started out. Aththai said hesitantly, 'Anna, please eat something before you leave.'

'No, 'ma. I had my fill at home before coming here.'

Mama wouldn't hear of it. 'It won't be proper if you leave without eating on visaakam day, machaan.'

'Why are you saying that, maapillai? Why should I object to eating? All of us have finished our meal. Chelambaram's mother was complaining that he hadn't eaten yet. I came here only to get away from her nagging. And this boy is loitering here after enjoying a free meal. And for this life of beggary, he is wearing a new shirt.'

Ayya left, muttering to himself. Janaki did not come out till he had crossed the doorstep.

Janaki was really scared of Ayya. She never came home when he was present. If by chance she peeped in through the door, he would frighten her with a round-eyed stare and protruding tongue. Sometimes he would catch her and make her cry. Then he would take her to the bazaar and buy her a lot of sweetmeats to appease her. Aththai would be overjoyed.

Ayya would complain: 'Why, the way my niece is behaving, it looks like she won't feed me gruel in my final years.'

Aththai would laugh at this too.

Janaki was normally vivacious and talked freely with Chidambaram. They walked to school together, even played together. They would pick and eat tamarind flowers and its tender pods by the public tank. The way she screwed up her face when she bit into a tamarind pod and chewed on it was quite a sight; she would blend the sourness into her laughter.

He would challenge her to a contest. She should watch him eat tamarind fruit without screwing up her face. She had lost to him plenty of times.

It was a special treat to eat different types of mixed rice with Janaki in the front yard, under the moonlight. She would tease him as she ate. He would burst out laughing. He would choke on his food and cough loudly. Aththai would come running from inside the house and slap the back of his head. Janaki, though, would continue to eat as if nothing had happened.

Because of the milling crowds during visaakam, Janaki and Chidambaram were not allowed to go up the hill. Aththai had refused them permission. Janaki badly wanted to go. She had never climbed up the hill before. If she had been allowed to mingle freely with other children, she wouldn't have yearned for it so much.

People coming from distant villages had a hard time climbing up the hill. So the path to the temple was repaired. After climbing down, the travellers relaxed on the bank of the public tank. When she saw them, Janaki's desire grew even more intense.

Janaki, Chidambaram and his elder brother went there at night to look at the entertainment shows. Aththai had given them a lot of pocket money to buy treats.

Ayya had set out earlier. If he left bearing a staff, it meant that he would come back only at dawn. He would make the crowds sit down, and keep them from dispersing, so that the entertainment shows could go on.

Ayya worked at the ginning factory. Vadakkuraan's brother-in-law had started it as a new business in the town. He bought a good piece of land and put up a very large building with a high compound wall, like a fortress. He had run a commission agency earlier. After his marriage to Vadakkuraan's sister, some other person was appointed to look after the shop. Next to the commission agency, they set up a shop for selling cotton seeds. Mama and Vadakkuraan's brother-in-law enjoyed a comfortable relationship. The owner had requested

Mama to sell the cotton from his fields to the factory and to canvass the cultivators in the neighbouring villages to do the same. Mama had agreed.

Ayya was recruited at the ginning factory because they needed an extra pair of hands. A large number of men from the street near the foothill worked in the factory. For a few hours daily, Ayya would scoop and gather the ginned cotton from the mill into piles; he spent the rest of the day loitering about.

For visaakam, Ayya received a brand-new dhoti and towel from the ginning factory.

Janaki and Chidambaram happily traipsed behind Annan. When she saw a karagam dancer, a woman, swivel her waist sharply, Janaki asked him, 'Won't her waist break in two, Chelambaram?'

In another place, a kuravan–kurathi dance accompanied by naiyaandi melam was being performed. Dramas sponsored by a few big bidi companies were performed at the temple junction. They didn't watch any of the acts to the end. When they were returning home, the programme on the radio was blaring above all the other noise.

Three days later, Janaki insisted stubbornly that she would come to the hill. No matter how much Aththai tried to convince her, she simply would not listen. Aththai relented finally and sent her with

Chidambaram. She remembered to give them flip-flops to wear for the trip.

Janaki ran eagerly to climb the hill. He didn't find climbing difficult. His main difficulty was taking her along. She started whining when they were halfway up the hill. 'Chelambaram, I want custard apple.'

She loved green custard apples. She would keep them like cowpeas in a pouch at her waist. She would whine and make such demands whenever there was no school. He wouldn't be able to face her if he didn't bring some for her.

'We'll go up and look for them.'

All along the route, she peeped into the caves. He kept scaring her till they reached the cave temple.

When she saw the cave temple, her cheerful mood vanished and her face shrank. How eager she had been at the entrance to the temple!

There were two statues inside the temple, of an adult man and a boy. The adult was grotesque to look at. He was wearing the boy's entrails around his neck. The boy lay on the ground, his belly torn open and bleeding, and the imprint of death upon his features. On another side, there was the statue of a woman looking at the two and laughing.

Janaki gripped his hand. He asked her, 'Why are you staring like that?'

She was still unable to speak. She wanted to leave. She didn't speak until both of them had reached the tamarind tree at the top.

When they sat down under the shade of the tree, she asked him, 'Why is it like that inside the temple, Chelambaram?'

'How would I know?'

'It's horrible.'

'I don't like it either.'

'That poor little boy. Why did they have to pull out his intestines?'

'There's a story they tell in the village. Don't you know it?'

'No.'

'The big man is the father and the boy is his son, it seems.'

'Tso, tso.'

'See that temple next to this one? Inside that temple, there was a half-done idol that the father would sculpt daily, they say. Every afternoon, the boy would bring him food from down below. When the father was sculpting, the son too picked up a chisel in the next temple and started sculpting in time with the taps of his father's chisel. So the father couldn't hear the sound of two chisels. One day, when the father stopped his work, he heard the sound of another

Poomani

chisel. He went out to look and found out that in the
neighbouring temple the boy had finished carving a
beautiful idol. The father became very angry. He tore
open his son's belly with the same chisel and wore the
boy's intestines around his neck.'

She closed her eyes with both hands. Then she
looked at him. 'Poor boy. Why should the father mind
if the son makes an idol?'

'The little boy had done a much better job than the
adult, see? That's why the father got angry.'

'Who made idols of these two, then?'

'The father himself did it, perhaps.'

Janaki didn't speak much after that. She seemed
unwell. They didn't go to the temple near the hilltop.

They peeped into another cave. Inside, a hermit
was sitting on a deerskin spread on a stone seat. His
eyes were closed. His head was full of grey hair. After
moving on from there, Janaki asked Chidambaram,
'Does that man sit here all the time?'

'Yes.'

'What will he do for food?'

'People who climb up the hill give him fruits and
milk. That's his food. If you go down a short distance
from here, there's a spring that never goes dry. He
bathes there.'

'He has matted hair. Won't he get it cut?'

'He never comes down from the hill.'

'Why should he live like this?'

'I don't understand it, either.'

When they climbed down to the foothill, Janaki didn't ask for custard apple. He wondered what had been the point of bringing her along.

She didn't go back to the hill a second time.

He still couldn't quite believe that Janaki had died. She had been laid up with fever for nearly four days, moaning terribly all night. One night was especially bad, with no one managing any sleep. He stayed awake too for a while, and then fell asleep. In the morning he woke up to the sound of people wailing. Janaki was no more.

Ayya let out a wail. Aththai lay inert in a corner like a stick of firewood pushed into the stove. Aaththa was sitting next to her. Mama had gone out of the house like a crazed man. Annan had gone looking for him.

After Janaki died, Chidambaram stopped going to school. His family tried very hard to persuade him. Ayya bullied him. They even starved him. Aththai took him away without anyone knowing and gave him food.

After nightfall the next day, he took all his books and threw them into the pond. He dropped stones on them till they sank. Finally, he sent a cardboard book cover skittering across the pond.

He didn't like lying around idly at home, so he went along with his brother to graze the goats; no one scolded him any more.

Herding goats on the hillside with his brother was pleasant work. All day long he could watch the hawks wheeling keenly above the hills as if they were searching for something; holler into the caves and enjoy the cascade of different echoes; look for the bulls that trudged slowly across the fields near the foothill. If he used a big plant as shade, he could run up and down the hill with the goats all day without feeling tired.

The goats were scattered all over the hillside. Annan never bothered about them. He would climb a tree, lie down on a branch and sing happily. He never asked Chidambaram to mind the goats. The metal pail in which he carried his lunch would be hanging from another branch of the tree. He remembered it only when he was hungry.

Chidambaram amused himself by rolling large stones down the rocky terrain. The temple pond at the foothill was clearly visible from above. Tiny figures moved about on the stone steps leading to the temple's sacred tank. A flock of pigeons was flying around the temple tower like specks in the distance. There was the public tank on the other side. Around it stood a

phalanx of trees as if they were guarding the water;
then, the street at the foothill, his house and Mama's
house; women carrying head-loads of timber for
matchsticks; sweet shops; people moving about at all
hours like black ants meeting, talking, parting and
scurrying away.

Annan hollered and called him for the midday
meal. 'Ei, Chelambaram. Bring the food pail and
come over!'

They went to the rock spring. Annan mashed the
rice into gruel, poured some for him in the lid of the
pail and drank up the rest. Water from the rock spring
tasted sweet, like coconut milk. If he drank a bit too
much, he had to lie in the shade till the dizziness
went away.

Chidambaram was amazed when all the goats
came together promptly at dusk. If Annan merely
whistled, the goats came running from wherever they
were. He had trained them to do so.

Chidambaram couldn't whistle like Annan. For
seven or eight days, Annan worked hard at teaching
him. By the time he got used to whistling, his mouth
ached and his lower jaw had swollen.

Annan could whistle in many different ways. He
whistled joining each finger by turns with his thumb
and also with each finger separately in his mouth.

He even whistled with a short stick placed across his tongue.

Annan did not allow the goats to enter another man's land. Whenever they were close to a cultivated field, his goats grazed in a disciplined way. If any goat reached out for a corn stalk and smelled it, he would simply say: '. . . ddhaa.' It was amazing how readily they obeyed that one word.

If they were caught on the hillside during rain, they had a hard time. If it was summer rain, the wind, too, would bother them. One day, while he was herding goats with Annan, they were caught in a cyclone.

Before the storm, the wind and rain carried a strong smell of earth. Annan asked him, 'Chelambaram, there's going to be a heavy downpour. Do you think we'll be able to bring the goats down?'

'Look at the mass of clouds. It'll start raining before we reach the foothill.'

'Wonder where the goats are. They'll scatter if the wind is high.'

'We'll collect the goats and settle them next to the compound wall of the temple.'

When they herded the goats and reached the hilltop, the wind had grown stronger. They watched the sky from inside the temple. The clouds were very dark. Rain descended on them like fine threads.

Daylight, which had remained hidden by the clouds, coloured the threads yellow. In their town, the weavers would stretch the warp in the mornings and apply dye to the threads. This rain was like a warp stood vertically on end.

The goats huddled together, shivering and expecting rain. Once the wind and rain arrived, they stopped grazing and wandered around restlessly.

Lightning streaked across the sky like an arc of red-hot wire; it was followed by a big thunderbolt. The goats squeezed against the wall. The wind blew fiercely. Lashed by the wind, the rain looked like the hair on a giant head, swinging this way and that.

Annan called to him eagerly.

'Come here, Chelambaram. See how that huge banyan tree on the roadside is twisting in the wind.'

The tree shook this way and that, as though it were pulled by ropes, and finally fell on its side, uprooted from the ground. A short while later, the entire roof of a house came flying off. It amused the boys to see it floating in the air.

Near the village, the gale had lifted a man and flung him in the air. Abandoning his usual route, he had walked along the path laid by the storm and managed to reach the village with some minor injuries.

Their mother was relieved when both of them

finally reached home along with the goats. The next day, the goats grazed on the banyan tree. It was easy for little boys to climb branch after branch and swing in the air or drive imaginary cars in it.

When Annan was grazing the goats, he would get really angry if anyone abused him. On that particular day, the goats were standing in a field next to Vadakkuraan's farm and grazing on fodder stalks cut down during harvest. The henchman from Vadakkuraan's farm came there and kicked up a row.

'Who is that brainless idiot grazing goats in a cultivated field? Do you eat rice or do you eat shit?'

Annan said, 'Watch that reckless talk. Complain if they had bitten off even a bit of your crop. There's no need to abuse.'

The thug was full of bluster.

'You wander into a cultivated field, and you talk about the law? Who do you think you are? If you don't get out now, I'll kill your goats and quarter the meat.'

Even a punk running errands in Vadakkuraan's farm was this arrogant. As if he was the one who carried his boss on his back! The fat thug knew Annan; he also knew Ayya. But it didn't stop him from spewing such reckless abuse.

Annan lost his patience.

'Just shut your face, man. You're talking as if this is your father's property. If my goats are grazing in the adjacent field, how can you call it robbery?'

The thug came running towards Annan.

'You trespass into our farmland and give me lip as well. Does your backside want a hiding?'

Annan didn't budge.

'Farmland, you say. When you grab everybody's land, does it become yours? Come near me if you dare, and you'll find out. Do you think I am a little boy?'

'Of course you'll talk. After all, you are the son of that Paramasivam who begs for food.'

'Why are you butting him in the shin? Aren't you forgetting that you shave your boss's private parts for a living? If you are smart, you should say this in front of my father. If he comes to know, he'll break your spine.'

'Why should I trade words with a little punk like you? If I tell the right people, they'll take care of everything.'

The thug walked away in a hurry.

Annan stewed in anger, unable to move from the field. 'He should have come closer. I don't think he could have walked away so fast.'

After the goats had grazed enough to fill their bellies, they returned home at dusk.

Annan didn't tell anyone at home about what had happened. He tethered the goats as usual, washed up and sat down to eat.

Chidambaram had already told them. Before Ayya could speak, Aaththa asked him angrily, 'And you let him go free? See how he is trying to get back at you!'

Ayya mumbled.

'That vannar[7] dog who has to sleep on top of the steaming pot is bragging about his power. It's time for him to die. I've been watching his behaviour. He comes and fawns over us, but speaks in a different tongue when our backs are turned.'

'What kind of man are you! You go out of your way to chit-chat with him.'

'That idiot comes over and talks to me. It's usually gossip about someone or the other in our village. I listen with one ear.'

'He is not such a pushover, is he? He doesn't like us owning land the size of a palm's width over there. He'll rest only after he has merged it with Vadakkuraan's farm.'

'I was looking out for him earlier today. I don't know when he is going to get clobbered.'

---

[7] of the washerman caste

Aaththa served a second portion of vegetables to Annan. He ate in silence. As she moved about inside the house, Aaththa kept swearing for a long time. Ayya finished eating and went out.

Their land was surrounded by Vadakkuraan's fields. He had bought up everything in their vicinity. Only their land was yet to be acquired by him. Vadakkuraan had sent word through his people many times. He was offering a good price for their land. Vadakkuraan spoke cordially to Ayya. Whenever he visited the ginning factory, he never failed to look him up.

One day, when Chidambaram carried food for Ayya, he found Vadakkuraan talking to Ayya. Finally Vadakkuraan said, almost in passing, 'Paramasivam, it will be great for us if you sell off this piece of land. Isn't it hard for you to come all the way and farm it? For me, it'll be part of the same job. The bull that ploughs my field has to take only a couple of more steps to plough yours.'

The ginning factory's owner looked at Ayya. 'He really wants it, as you can see. Why don't you just get rid of it? Why have one foot here and one foot there?'

Ayya demurred. 'We can give you the land, but I need to have a word with my brother-in-law.'

'I'll talk to him. You only have to give your consent.'

Ayya was evasive.

'Even so, it's land that he has gifted us. It's only proper that I should ask him personally.'

'No one is telling you not to. Go ahead and ask him. Let us know your decision soon.'

As Ayya was leaving, Vadakkuraan said, 'It'll do if you send word after you've talked to everyone.'

When Ayya broached the topic with him, Mama didn't want to sell. 'We need to own some land. Only then would we want to work like the others. Hold on to it. I'll help you farm that land.'

Ayya still sounded bitter. 'Maapillai, for how long can we keep a bone in front of a dog? We'll end up having to fight these bastards forever. When I lived off my own land in my village, it ended in murder. It looks like the same thing might happen here.'

'Machaan, how can you talk like this? You could have given up the land in your village and spent your life collecting dung in the owner's house. If that's the way you feel, why should we bother with postures and negotiations?'

'I would rather beg than work for him, maapillai. Do you think I would ever enter his house? I'll hide my sickle inside a begging bowl, lure him to the street and hack him.'

'Look at this land in the same way. Are we causing

him any trouble? He might commit a thousand atrocities. Why should *we* succumb to him?'

'His talk is too intense. I don't know where it will lead. We'll wait and see. We won't start a fight on our own, nor will we walk away if a fight comes our way.'

'I like the way you're talking now.'

Mama's bulls were put to work on their land also. They were entitled to draw water from Vadakkuraan's well.

Vadakkuraan had a power connection at the well to run a pump set. They had no share in the power because Ayya wouldn't agree to it. Their farming was done by drawing water with a cattle-drawn water lift.

During periods of water scarcity, Vadakkuraan would suck up all the water from the well. The water lift could not be used. Ayya would get angry and shout, 'Shouldn't they know that the crop in the neighbour's field is parched? If they won't leave us our share, there'll be hell to pay. I'll smash the pump set and lay it in a corner.'

To avoid any conflict, Vadakkuraan dug another well next to the existing one and established a power connection. But water eluded the new well. It turned out to be a waste of money.

Vadakkuraan had undertaken dryland cultivation

in several fields. He had no water entitlement for
those fields. When he transported water from their
shared well, Ayya stopped him. 'I won't let you carry
a drop of water. If you want, you should dig a well
there too.'

Again there was an argument. The ill-feeling
spread to the ginning factory. Slyly, the owner asked
Ayya, 'If you're so aggressive with your little patch of
land, think how others might have to behave.'

Ayya didn't hold back. 'They can behave in any way
they are able to. But why should they be allowed to
kick people around?'

'All right. But shouldn't you show some basic
courtesy?'

'Speak generally and say that everyone should.'

'Of course I am speaking generally. If you want to
act this way, others will also start raising their voices.
The trouble this man is facing today could be ours
tomorrow.'

After overhearing their conversation, Chidambaram
returned home worried.

The chat led to the end of Ayya's job. After that
day, he stopped going to the ginning factory. He had
a word with Mama, who didn't try to dissuade him.
Ayya said with finality, 'What kind of life is this,

maapillai? If we continue to have dealings with him, it will be a permanent headache.'

Mama said gently, 'As you wish.'

After leaving his job at the ginning factory, Ayya tended his land very well. Mama was happy that instead of roaming around with his stick in hand, Ayya was focusing on his work. He said proudly to Aaththa, 'The way machaan is working, he might buy up all of Vadakkuraan's lands.'

Aaththa wasn't so sure.

'I am sure he would want that to happen, but I'll be happy if he just holds on to what we have today.'

As the days went by, even the interaction between the ginning factory owner and Mama was much reduced. They didn't speak often like they used to earlier. Cotton from Mama's farm was sold to someone else. When the old village headman asked him, Mama replied wearily, 'He doesn't like to see us in decent clothes. It makes him fret and fume. If a man gives in to collective pressure from everyone, he is a good man; otherwise, he is a rogue.'

'That's not the only reason. You also mediate local disputes. And he grudges you that.'

'What can we do about it? Should we sit at home just because he mediates disputes? If he is arbitrary and unfair, how does he expect people to put up with it?'

'But there are always a bunch of men with him, living off his crumbs.'

'That's right.'

Mama settled a lot of disputes in the village. People came from other villages in the area to invite him for mediation. He wasn't loud and overbearing like Ayya. He would listen carefully to all parties and then speak his mind.

Ayya was different. If he didn't like something, he would become really angry. Clutching his stick, he would get up and leave the gathering. This had happened several times on the bank of the public tank.

Mama had good relations with many influential men. He spoke to the rich landlords with self-possession. They listened to him.

He didn't like Ayya's behaviour. He would speak impartially and courteously to everyone. He didn't hold a stick in his hand. He carried only a sheathed armlet tucked into his waist.

Mostly he didn't take Ayya along when he went for his resolutions. Ayya also stopped going with him.

Mama had settled a very large number of land disputes in the surrounding villages without entailing any litigation expenditure for the parties. Some came to him after getting tired of trudging to the courts for many years. He never levied penalties on anyone. He would get both parties to exchange a round of betel leaves and arrive at a settlement. He refused to mediate some disputes, no matter how much pressure was brought on him. He would get angry if he heard of cases that involved the ending of a marital bond.

'Is it my job to destroy another man's family? You should have united the two families yourself; you've come to invite me instead, what kind of man are you? Don't you have a sister? If anyone tries to interfere in this matter, there'll be hell to pay. Get lost and mind your own business. That family will come together on its own.'

Stunned, the man would go away meekly. Mama would let the matter cool for some time; then he would go to their village, give them personal advice and unite the family.

Many people were angry with Mama over the money aspect. They were angry because he was spoiling the potential income of some big landlords who also did such work.

They usually heard a case over two or three days, causing sizeable expense to the disputants, levied large penalties and even claimed a share of such amounts. They were experts on brokerage matters in disputes involving sales of cattle at the cattle fair.

But they spoke pleasantly to Mama whenever they met him. Mama's participation in settling cases had provoked hatred even among the local police. They stood to lose their income, didn't they? They had called Mama one day and warned him.

Aththai lamented often, 'Why do we need this trouble? Why should these fights between strangers land in our house? It can't be that only you can resolve them. There are many big men around here who can do that.'

Mama would tell her, 'So you say. What unnecessary trouble? Are we inviting it? Shouldn't there be a limit to the atrocities these big men commit? If the landlords levy big fines on wage labourers and swindle their earnings, how will their families survive? If we try to put an end to this practice, these landlords get a sprain in the groin. Those government fellows are even worse. All thieves, working hand-in-glove! And you call them great souls. Great souls, my foot.'

When Aththai came to Ayya and complained, he made up lame excuses. 'How can I say anything to maapillai? He is not up to any monkey business, is he? Anyone who goes to argue a case before him can't even get a drink of water. That's the only thing I find wrong.'

Aththai was disappointed. She went away, moaning to herself. Aaththa shouted at Ayya. 'What kind of man are you? She is feeling hurt. Instead of saying a couple of soothing words, you talk foolishly and send her away.'

Ayya scratched his head in bemusement. Aaththa went looking for Aththai.

4

They had passed four or five villages in the east. But they hadn't found the right place. The ones they had come across were too accessible to passers-by.

They found a bridge on a village road. There, just as the day was beginning, three people had spread a towel and were playing a game of cards. Ayya was furious.

'Don't these fellows have a home and family? I am so angry I want to drop a big rock on each one's head. See how they've settled here even before daylight!'

They stopped beside a stream. There were a few betel gardens on the opposite bank. Ayya stuck out his lip in disappointment.

'The owner would have planted thorn trees all around and fenced off the area. It's like an upturned chicken coop, a good place if you want to get caught.

The owner will no doubt be hovering near that fence all the time.'

A short distance away, they saw a field of lush sugar cane. To the north ran a trunk road, and on its left was a village bypass road; beyond that lay the cane field; past the cane field, a village.

Ayya walked towards the bypass road. Mama was to meet them there.

Chidambaram stepped inside the cane field. Half the field was well irrigated and the other half was dry. In the wet half, he dipped his feet in the main channel and then walked along its course, cross-stepping alternately on both ridges to obscure his tracks. After crossing a field, he stood on a grassy ridge at the border and listened for sounds.

It wouldn't be wise to stay in the middle of a field. If he were surrounded, there would be no way to escape.

He turned southward and sat below a ridge along which sugar cane had been planted. Moving the cane stalks out of the way, he levelled a patch of ground on the ridge. If he ran south from that spot, he would enter a wooded area. No one could find him there. Since that part of the field was already watered, it was unlikely that anyone would come there.

He sat confidently on the ridge and waited

for Mama's arrival. He had settled there without informing them beforehand about the spot. How could they possibly know? Before leaving, Ayya, too, hadn't told him to wait in any particular spot. Ayya would have done it deliberately, in order to case the surroundings. He might sit on the western side and keep a watch over the area.

As he waited, Chidambaram heard a rustling sound nearby. Kneeling in the slush, an enormous wild pig was eating cane stalks. It had drooping, fat jowls and very long canine teeth. As it spat out the sugar cane refuse, it appeared as though the pig was laughing hideously. It paused with an inward growl.

It must have escaped somehow from the hillside. No dog could capture it. The pig had merely to sink its canines into the dog to lift it up.

The pig wouldn't be disturbed by stone throwing. If it was struck squarely in the temple, it might keel over. Else, you had to plunge a sickle deep into the neck. The entire sickle would sink into the flesh and couldn't be pulled out. If, noticing the raised sickle, the pig crushed it with its canine teeth, the sickle would splinter into many pieces.

Chidambaram's own sickle was damaged by Vadakkuraan. His body had been all beef and muscle. The flesh hardened into rock. What had he done to build his body like that? Chidambaram wondered.

His hand was hesitant when he first picked up the sickle. As he raised his arm above the shoulder, he had felt a surge of fear. But once he struck the man, his fear had vanished. With the two bombs in his hand, he had nothing to be afraid of.

He could bring this pig down by throwing a bomb at it. But what would he achieve by killing the wretched creature? It would give off a horrible stench. If the noise from the bomb's explosion was heard, it would only lead to more trouble. The pig with its toothy grin could be gored with a spear staff. It would simply thrust its tongue out and keel over.

He didn't know the men who had pursued him the other night. They had escaped by a hair's breadth. Else, with his aim, they should have been blown to bits. It was their good fortune that the bus had arrived just then and he couldn't take out the other bomb. If he had stepped away from the road in the dark, they would have continued running. What if he had called out, 'Run, machaan,' from behind their backs? Why had they chased him like blind fools?

For Vadakkuraan, however, the time of reckoning had come. He had shoved dirt into the mouths of so many people, robbed them of their livelihoods, and now he had bitten the dust himself. By now, goats must be grazing the grass over his grave. Why did his pursuers care that Vadakkuraan had got his due? It was ridiculous. When Mama comes, I must ask him about those two rogues.

Making the bombs had been no small matter. How hard he had worked to make them – with a lot of effort, he had collected gunpowder, picked porcelain bits from factory waste, bought nails and put them together. He had indeed gone to a lot of trouble.

He had pestered Aaththa for some cooked millet. After giving him the once-over, she asked him, 'What's this new craze, elei?'

'Nothing, Aaththa. Just craving millet.'

'Why this craving that you've never had before?'

'Just like that. What am I going to do with cooked millet, anyway?'

'You can hold on in that case. I'll cook it some other day.'

'You *have* to do it for me today.'

'Then tell me what it's about.'

There was no escaping from Aaththa.

'Want to try putting together a couple of . . .'

'That's a lot better. Assembling is fine, but do you know all the details? Otherwise, you'd be asking for trouble.'

'I do.'

'As you wish, then. Do it carefully. Why do you need them, though?'

'Only for safety.'

'You are right, son. You should always carry weapons. My boy had no weapon on the day he was killed. If he had been armed, who would've dared to go near him?'

Aaththa cooked a pot of millet for him with the right texture. He cured it by making it into a paste, smearing the paste on a cloth and drying it in the sun.

Chidambaram moved past without disturbing the pig, who was busy gorging on sugar cane. Mongooses slipped by like slender threads. Wild cats leapt about, chasing their prey. Seeing him, they stopped, their eyes glowing like hot coals.

Near the ridge on the western border, he pushed the sugar cane stalks aside and looked out. Mama and Ayya were walking together. They didn't proceed directly to the cane field. They turned and walked towards a cluster of palm trees on the bank of the stream. He went over to them.

Mama's appearance had changed. He had stubble on his face and looked unwell. He never looked shabby. He always had a close shave, making his moustache stand out impressively. Today though his normal glow was missing. He was feeling sad, perhaps.

Chidambaram wished that his family didn't have to face all this trouble.

Mama sat leaning against the palm tree. Chidambaram sat down next to him. Ayya was thinking deeply about something. The boy leaned back on Mama's lap. Mama rested his arm on Chidambaram.

'Chelambaram, so thin you've become in just two or three days!'

'I've wanted to tell you the same thing.'

'What, me? I only eat and hang around at home.'

'You stay at home, do you? I know everything.'

'What do you know?'

'That you're making Aththai run around.'

Mama patted his back.

'Aththai is really worried about you, boy. If you want her to bring food here for you, she will.'

'Poor Aththai, why do you make her run around?'

'Aren't we all running around?'

'All because of me.'

Ayya, who had been thinking about something, lowered his eyes. Mama pressed his arm on Chidambaram even harder. Ayya said in a normal voice, 'It's because of me, son.'

He looked skyward as before. Mama intervened. 'We're all to blame. Why talk about it now? Eat first and we can discuss the rest later. Chelambaram, will you eat what Aththai has packed for you? Or will you give me what you've cooked?'

Chidambaram stood up. Ayya's face betrayed no sense of hurt.

'Mama, you should spend a whole day and see for yourself. Then you'll know whether I can cook or not. You've come at the wrong time today. Have you had your food?'

'I'm done. You two go ahead and come back.'

Taking the bag from Mama, Ayya asked him, 'The packet looks big. Why don't you come along and eat something, maapillai?'

'To give you company, is it?'

Ayya and Chidambaram got up and went to the well nearby. After setting aside a portion for their lunch, they finished their meal and came back quickly.

Mama kept talking till it was afternoon. Mostly, he spoke about the case. 'The police have filed the case. The work's proceeding really well, they say.'

Ayya nodded his head. 'Why wouldn't it? It's the least they can do after living off Vadakkuraan for so long. They hate us, and that's one more reason. Who all are charged, then?'

'Only you and Chelambaram. I am surprised they didn't include me.'

'There must be a reason. They would know it, obviously. After all, it is they who sit around all night, every night, cooking up the case. Is the autopsy over?'

'Yes, it's done.'

'Their witnesses must be ready.'

'The stall owner is one. Another is that henchman from Vadakkuraan's house.'

'Just perfect for the case. What will they say in court?'

'That Vadakkuraan and his thug were buying things at the stall. Both of you went there and snatched money from them. The row turned into a fight. You cut Vadakkuraan with a sickle, threw a bomb and killed him. Then you took off. That's their case. They'll ask these two to back that story.'

'A clever story, maapillai. Adding you would've made the story even better; that's why he's left you out. Did he get someone to write the report, or did he cook it up himself?'

'Our village massif wrote it.'

'The cheek!'

'When he is told to write it, what else can he do?'

'Not really, maapillai. He is not so guileless. A quiet schemer. They're all in it together, the scoundrels!'

Chidambaram was surprised. He asked Mama,

'What exactly was Vadakkuraan's thug supposed to be doing when all this happened?'

Ayya was annoyed. 'Must have plucked and chewed tamarind pods.'

Mama said, 'He got scared and ran away.'

'How did the police find out about us, Mama?'

'Someone saw your father running into the alley for cover. They worked it out from there.'

'And those two guys who came running after me? I thought they must have told on us. Did you find out who they were, Mama?'

'Just a couple of coolies in the market. They're known to us. One got away unhurt. The other was wounded in one leg. He didn't go to the hospital, though – got it bandaged privately.'

'This must be a lucky period for him.'

'I scolded them both. They stood quietly with their heads down. Would they have chased you if they had known the background?'

'As if anyone would tell them beforehand.'

Mama looked at Ayya, who was still wrapped up in his thoughts. He asked Mama after a brief pause, 'Did you find out about the case details through the advocate?'

'No. There's a policeman who is a good friend of mine, as you know.'

'That means they'll draw up the charge sheet very soon.'

'That's good for us. The case will go forward without a hitch.'

'You said the dog was brought in.'

'Yes, it came. It ran south from the murder spot and stopped cold on the street leading to the cattle fairground.'

'Then it would have lifted a hind leg and peed on its handler.'

'You made a mistake, turning and running on the street.'

'True, I shouldn't have. What could I do? I was in a hurry. I had fixed the transformer. I didn't want anyone to see that the fuse had been pulled out. I had to come home and send your sister away. Only after I reached the temple did I realize that I shouldn't have run away. While I was running, I saw a security constable at the entrance to the police station. He must have recognized me.'

'It's possible. When all this was going on, the head constable and I were standing at the tea stall near the temple, drinking tea.'

'Were you? That's why they didn't include you in the charge sheet, perhaps. But they are never honest, though. Once they were bribed, I am sure they would have harassed our families.'

'In your house, they ripped out the front door and kept it outside, smashed a few roof tiles above the veranda. Little by little, we had gradually taken away all the household items and dumped them in my house. When they went there, my wife slipped away to the neighbours'. They didn't do any damage to the house. They called the village headman and questioned him. He managed somehow to send them away.'

'How can we be on the run forever? It means hardship for all of you. How are things in the village? A big crowd must have come from Vadakkur when the corpse was handed over . . . no other incident, right?'

'Yes, a few fellows turned up. That ginning factory owner! The man was swaggering around. The boys from our street were also fully armed, ready to face any move. No one would have dared to provoke us.'

'Did they bury the body in our village or take it to Vadakkur?'

'They took it away in a covered bullock cart.'

'It couldn't have been a corpse in that cart. They must have broken the skull open like a palm fruit and removed the brain, cut the belly open and pulled out the intestines. They might have rolled up the rest in a palm-leaf mat like a packet of tamarind and handed it to them. That ginning factory owner ought to have met the same fate the other day. So, why wouldn't he act big now?'

'Right. He is still just as arrogant.'

'Arrogant, my foot! He would rather unleash a couple of his errand boys and watch the fun than go anywhere near a fight.'

'It's a disaster we've brought on ourselves.'

'That's right. Had our people joined that procession, would he have dared to pick up a gun?'

'And he killed an innocent fellow who was just driving his bullock cart – it makes my blood boil whenever I think about it.'

'We should have cut his meat and fed it to the crows that day. Now he is riding around on his motorcycle like a big, black buffalo, with a cigarette dangling from his lips. We'll see how long this lasts.'

Ayya gnashed his teeth in anger.

'Chelambaram, are you feeling sleepy?'

Mama pinched his thigh.

'How can I sleep when I'm thinking of that man? I was recalling that incident.'

'You saw it with your own eyes, didn't you?'

'What difference does it make? He killed a man in front of so many people, and now he moves around like an innocent man, with a bunch of toadies following him. I feel so angry when I see that lot.'

Chidambaram straightened his spine and leaned back. Ayya said spitefully, 'Let him strut, son. Some day, someone will surely do away with him. It'll be Vadakkuraan's story all over again. But what about all those landlords who went with their carts in a procession that day? Now, they sell him their cotton and drink coffee with him. That makes me really angry.'

'Even that doesn't trouble me, machaan. The servant who loads the cotton on his bullock cart and delivers it there, even he doesn't seem to be bothered. That's really sad.'

'Even if he is, what can he do? If he goes there with a sickle, the guard will snatch it away and send him back.'

'Killing that black beast will settle the score, Mama.'

'That murderer is leading a comfortable life. The police haven't laid a finger on him. They haven't even filed a case for show.'

'Didn't Vadakkuraan do the same?'

'But they are chasing our arse for killing him, aren't they?'

Ayya butted in, 'We've been fighting this injustice forever, maapillai.'

Chidambaram was angry.

'Then we must fix them all together. It only seems fair. What do you say, Mama?'

Mama said, 'What can the police do? There are so many cursed things above them, like law and procedure.'

'Does the law tell you to kill unjustly? Or does it push you to have a good time with the killer?'

Chidambaram looked at Mama and Ayya. They did not speak. Mama scratched his chin. Ayya was drawing some twigs through a web of palm fibre to clean them.

The heat began to rise.

Mama set out after midday. Chidambaram made sure to send some resin with him. Aththai loved resin. She would remove the crusted outer layer, warm up the juicy white core and eat it. Melted with palm sugar, it tasted like honey. She would eat it hot off the stove.

Ayya returned after seeing Mama off. There was a portion left over from the rice that Mama had given them. Chidambaram sat against the tree with the food packet lying next to him. Ayya sat under an adjacent palm tree.

'Do we have to eat this afternoon, son? We just ate and can't feel hungry so soon.'

'We'll keep what's left over for the night.'

'Why is your arm swollen? What happened? Here, let me see it.'

'I was stung by a honeybee yesterday.'

'Adada. Is that why it's swollen and shiny? Has the stinger come out? I hadn't noticed it. You must find it difficult to hold anything.'

'It was just a tiny hook. I took it out. The swelling will go down by tomorrow.'

'You're such a crazy boy.'

'Did Mama tell you anything?'

'He scolded me. He thinks I am not taking proper care of you.'

'What can you do when we are both stuck in the middle of nowhere?'

'I told him, "If you think the going is bad now, what will happen if they convict us and put us in jail? There'll be no talk of good food then."'

'So his main worry is food, is it? Who is going to give us good food in jail, our grandfather?'

'We should arrest all those who work there and lock them up first. There's nothing they wouldn't do. They gobble up all the milk and fruit and meat, and the prisoners get only what's left . . . It feels like it all happened yesterday.'

Sitting with both palms planted on the ground

behind him, Ayya was looking upward. His gaze seemed to have conjured something taller than a palm tree.

Keeping his eyes on his father, Chidambaram said, 'If it was such a farce then, it will be a lot worse now.'

Ayya didn't seem perturbed. With his gaze in the far distance, he said, 'There was an old man with me. He was of stocky build. I was very young then, just a bit older than you are now.' He lowered his gaze and looked intently at Chidambaram.

'Why was he put in jail?'

'He had come in for a couple of murders. He took good care of me. He hated people who were in jail for theft and robbery. He beat them up openly. What was I telling you . . .? They gave us gruel one day. It was always lumpy. The mush they gave the old man had a strand of hair. He pulled the hair out and used it to divide the mush into four slices. He was furious.'

'Did he throw it away?'

'No. Controlling his anger, he smiled at me and put the glob in his mouth. Otherwise, I wouldn't have eaten that gruel.'

'How many years was he in for?'

'He was convicted for two murders; so he was sentenced for life. He wasn't afraid of punishment.

"What do I need now? It's enough if my children do well. It doesn't matter where I am," he would say and go off to sleep. That kind of grit doesn't come easy to anyone. Many people came to visit him. He always shared the food they passed secretly to him with me.'

'Sounds like a nice man.'

'He was really happy when I was released. I felt sad leaving him. My eyes began to tear up. He gave me a pep talk and saw me off.'

Ayya sighed. Chidambaram was watching him.

'Did you visit him after you came out?'

'I met him in jail twice, after filing an application each time. He even wrote me letters, but not for long because I didn't stay put anywhere. On the day he was released, I bought him a dhoti and towel set. His head was white like a bale of cotton, but his strength was intact. He had gone inside before me.'

'Where was he from?'

'From the southern tracts. After your mother and I married, we lost all contact. He must have passed away by now. Even today, I feel sad when I think of that man.'

'Even such a good man had to go to jail.'

'His enemies had got together and planned to destroy his family. He was watching. Till his children were able to stand on their own feet, he allowed himself to be pushed around. Once they were settled, he killed a couple of his enemies and headed for jail.'

'So much rage.'

'No ordinary rage. He roasted one victim's bone and ate it. That's how angry he was.'

'God knows what they did to him.'

'There's never a shortage of injustice, right? If there's a northerner tormenting us today, there was a southerner in the past.'

'And it's we who end up in jail.'

Ayya laughed and eased his body on to the ground. 'In jail, no one worried much about food. But they'd die for a bidi. If a man got hold of a bidi, he'd save it as if it was mutton curry and savour it for a long time. He would save up his daily allotment of groundnuts and get someone to buy him bidis in exchange. If his neighbour had bidis, he would trade his groundnuts for a bidi. Some men sold off even their food.'

'They were so addicted.'

'One morning we were being herded outside like cattle. Some people were carrying their urine pots as they walked. On the way, a bidi butt was lying on the ground. One prisoner picked it up with his toes. The jailer who was our minder noticed it. He made the prisoner squat down and kicked him in the ear.

The man who was squatting spun dizzily and toppled over. The old man was really angry. He warned the jailer that he would be torn apart if he touched anyone again. The injured man also received an earful. From that day on, no one was beaten in that jail. The jailers would grumble and mutter to themselves when they saw the old man, but it was all they could do.'

'So, beating up people who are locked up is a smart move, is it?'

'It must seem like a smart move to them,' said Ayya wearily. He stretched out again. Then he sat up and lit a bidi, and rubbed his back on the palm tree.

Chidambaram said gently, 'We must get back to the sugar cane field in time. We have to scout for a place to sleep. If it gets dark and we can't find a good spot, the cane leaves will poke us all night. The wind has started already. It'll gather force with every passing hour. Let's head there quickly. What do you say?'

'We'll finish our meal and leave. We are not going to sleep in the middle of the field, are we? We'll sleep close to the edge, inside the channel. Then we can get away easily.'

'A wild pig is moving about in there.'

'Really? It must be doing a lot of damage.'

'It's gorging on the cane crop.'

'Once it gets a taste, it won't leave so easily.'

'If it's loitering on one side, we'll lie in another.'

'Won't the police come after us at night? If they are tipped off, they might come in a gang.'

'If they come, they'll get what's coming to them.'

'West of here, near my village, a fellow was on the lam, dodging a warrant. A whole gang of policemen had surrounded him in broad daylight. Each of them had a rifle. What was that man to do? It was his bad luck that some shit-eating stooge had squealed on him. He knew that if he was captured, they wouldn't take him alive. He decided that he would take out one guy before they got him. While running, he flung his sickle at one of them. It plunged into the man's shoulder blade. He tried to run, but couldn't get away. A policeman stood next to him and shot him down.'

'Was he hiding without a bomb?'

'If he had had one, the story would've been different.'

'If they come after us, we'll take out one policeman with each bomb. If we are killed after that, so be it.'

Ayya stood up.

'I'll roam around for a bit and come back. If it gets late, we can't scout for a suitable place to stay in for tomorrow. I've never been in these parts before. In an unfamiliar area, it's always good to have a look around.'

'True. We can't look for a hideout while we're on the move.'

'Are you staying here or going over to the cane field?'

'Don't worry about me. Come to the well by sunset. We will finish our meal and head over there.'

'Let's do that.'

Ayya started out. Chidambaram hid the food packet behind a bush at the foot of the palm tree. He didn't like the prospect of having nothing at all to do until sunset. After cutting down a useless fellow, he now had to run around uselessly.

All the trouble was caused only by the layabouts. He got so angry when he thought of their antics. Everyone bragged and bullied in their own way, creating endless trouble.

There were many political parties in the village. People swore their loyalty to one leader; later, they switched to his rival. They erected poles everywhere, all painted a different colour, and hoisted party flags. They tried to mount one flag higher than another. It was quite a spectacle in front of the temple ground. When it was windy, all the flags swayed and danced like demons.

Party meetings were held frequently in the village. The ginning factory owner spoke majestically at those meetings. Under the stage lights, his white bush shirt was a perfect match for his dark-skinned body. He always had a crowd around him. If a row or skirmish broke out later in the bazaar or on the main road, that meeting was the most probable cause.

Others muttered to themselves. 'Who can question him? His party is in power, so he is running wild.'

All parties held meetings in street junctions around the village and attacked one another. 'Don't I know your true colours; I'll expose you,' they would declaim passionately. The very next day, both men would be drinking tea together.

Some politicians abused the rich indiscriminately. Later, the same politicians visited their shops with collection boxes. It was truly a comic sight.

One evening, a big meeting was held in the village. People had come in large numbers from the surrounding villages. It was like the crowds at the annual visaakam festival. The roads were teeming with people; vehicles couldn't pass through. There were rows upon rows of bullock carts, filled with people. Everyone was holding a placard in their hands. A variety of slogans were inscribed on those placards.

Tractors had come from the houses of the rich

landlords. They went ahead of the bullock carts in the procession.

Policemen lined both sides of the road. The big leaders marched at the head of the procession, shouting slogans. As the leaders shouted each slogan, the people who followed behind repeated them. The leaders clenched their fists and raised them high. Some held flags aloft. They were dressed in oversize shirts and had a towel draped across their shoulder.

Chidambaram had often seen those big leaders in the company of the ginning factory owner. They would sit cross-legged in front of him and chat in a relaxed manner.

Enjoying the sights, he ran alongside the procession. He climbed the roadside trees and took in the splendour of the passing cars. There was talk that no bullock carts had come from villages like Vadakkur. Many reasons were mentioned. The meeting had been organized by one political party and the people who had kept away belonged to another.

The procession started in the street that led to the cattle fairground and proceeded towards the ginning factory. They had to take that route to go to the temple ground, their eventual destination.

The crowd marched forward in orderly rows,

looking like a field in a model farm, with a name tag attached to each plant. As the day progressed the noise from the crowds grew louder and louder. They now screamed without restraint. Those in the bullock carts stood up and shouted fierce slogans with raised fists.

A smaller crowd stood in front of the ginning factory. They shouted back in response. The people in the bullock carts were enraged. They shifted the placards from hand to hand while screaming abuses. Two women in a bullock cart who were chewing betel leaves and enjoying the spectacle suddenly extended their hands towards the ginning factory and cracked their knuckles in a spiteful gesture. Meanwhile, stones were pelted from the ginning factory. A few fell on the bulls. The bulls halted abruptly to show their displeasure.

Chidambaram clambered up a big neem tree and hid himself; from there, he watched the drama.

Incensed, the people in the bullock carts jumped down. They, too, started pelting stones. Stones rained down on the ginning factory and the house next to it. The policemen charged the roadside mob with lathis and drove them away.

Stone pelting from the other side grew more intense. Occasionally, some stones fell on the neem tree as well. He clung to the branch like a garden lizard. A very large number of people had collected in the area.

Several people tried to enter the ginning factory. The crowd that had started the stone pelting took refuge inside the factory and locked the gates. The factory owner stormed out of his house and threatened the crowd, wagging a finger at them; then he hurried inside and peeked through a window. A short while later, a series of explosions was heard.

A man driving a bullock cart screamed, 'Aiyaiyo, Amma!' and fell face down on the cart's frame. The crowd scattered in all directions. What happened to the leaders who had marched in front, shouting slogans? What happened to the policemen?

Chidambaram hurriedly got down from the tree and sprinted down the shortcut across the fields to his house.

He couldn't sleep at all that night. Ayya and Aaththa spoke for a long time about the incident.

The next day, there was a strained atmosphere in the town. There were crowds everywhere. All the shops were shut. In some shops, people watched the street from inside through half-open shutters. There were no people on the streets, only policemen.

A large contingent of policemen was standing guard around the ginning factory. In some places, leaders wearing oversize shirts and towels on their shoulders were pacifying enraged party workers.

Carrying the cart driver's corpse, the mourners marched quietly along the village streets. Many floral garlands were placed on the body. It wasn't clear why they had marched in silence. The leaders, who had gone ahead of the bullock carts the previous day, shouting slogans, marched now in front of the body with their heads bowed. The crowd followed them along the same route.

The dead man, it was said, used to work in the home of a big landlord in a neighbouring village. He had four or five children. Poor man. He had to come to work that day, he needed the money. Why did they shoot a man who was only driving a bullock cart? What could he have done? If he drove the cart, the owner would pay him a day's wage. He must have started from his village in the morning. They must have bought him lunch too.

An uproar began in the town. People gathered everywhere and discussed the case among themselves. The leaders held party meetings at night. At each meeting, they made speeches threatening the ginning factory owner. They found fault with the policemen.

It looked like the factory owner was going to get his due. One speaker even had his weapon ready and promised that he would finish off the villain once the speech was over. Gesturing with his hands and feet, he spoke with unbridled passion even as his tongue went dry and he stumbled, unable to speak further. After drinking a bottle of soda at the end of his speech, his temper cooled and he sat down peacefully, like a fire doused with water. It took a long time for the crowd's applause to subside.

Members of each party claimed that the dead man had belonged to their party. This led to a dispute. Therefore, one party had to find fault with the other. Finally, it was accepted that the dead man had been a member of one particular party.

Two months passed. Members of that party installed rows and rows of fluorescent lights in the temple ground and held a big meeting. The banners were especially abundant at the road junctions. The meeting was as colourful as the visaakam festival.

A tall leader from the remote north had come to address the meeting. He unveiled a marble-like stone pillar erected at the southern end of the temple ground. The name of the leader who unveiled it was inscribed prominently on the pillar.

As the days passed, people took to peeing behind the cover of that pillar at night. On market days, arrack was sold there.

There was no dearth of arrack in the village. They were selling it in tins. To some, it was a full-time occupation and it had made them rich. They also sold it in other villages, near and far. It often led to fights between villages in the area.

Black babul plants had grown abundantly in the fields, in dense thickets, making it easy for those who wanted to use it as fuel to distil arrack. Villagers harvested the black babul plant, burnt the wood to make charcoal and sold it as fuel. But there was little or no money in it. Money earned from selling charcoal was spent on meals in the eateries. Then they pledged future supplies of charcoal and ate on credit.

Now, the liquor vats were boiling on the stove along with the wood fires for making charcoal. Two people served as lookouts while they tended to the charcoal fires. A short distance away, the distillation of arrack went on.

Chidambaram, too, went to the liquor distillation facility one day. He had gone on a playful whim. All along the bank of the pond, pots for fermenting toddy lay buried like mushrooms sprouting on the ground.

They asked him to fetch water. He walked back and forth from the pond for many hours, carrying water for the vats. It felt like a children's game. It was fun to watch.

After keeping the vat for a few hours on the stove, they removed it, took out the wide-mouthed bowl that was hung inside and poured the arrack which had collected in it into two bottles and kept them separately. It was the first yield of the day. Then the vat was coated again with clay and set on the stove for the next round.

A couple of policemen in plain clothes came by and collected both the bottles from the first yield. They also drank some. Then they left, nibbling on the snacks they had brought with them.

Bootleggers went into hiding whenever they saw policemen, not from fear of being apprehended but because they couldn't afford to serve them free arrack. The policemen also had to be given money to feast on meat dishes in the eateries. Besides, monthly tributes had to be paid. In comparison, if a case was booked, it ended with mere penalty. Even after pampering them so much, the bootleggers in the area had to, by turns, present the policemen with two cases of arrack every month.

In spite of all these expenses, there was still profit to be made in the arrack business. Otherwise, how could a man given to useless loitering end up with a ring on every finger? This was why the neem and babul trees in the fields were stripped bare of their bark and branches. Even small plants were not spared.

Now the distillery business had advanced further. Instead of removing the collector pot from the stove, the trade employed a new technique to draw the distilled arrack directly through a pipe into a bottle.

On the day Chidambaram went to the distillery, he got a full tumbler from the final yield of the day. He closed his eyes and swallowed it. The nausea was unbearable. On the way back, he had to lie down under a bridge. He retched till his guts ached. When he resumed walking after dunking his head and bathing in the stream, he was ashamed. It was the end of his drinking. Luckily, Mama didn't get to know about it.

Drinking arrack had horrible consequences. Kaarmegam lost an arm because of his drinking. He was married to the headman's daughter. They had two children. He once used to look so smart when he set out daily on his bicycle for his job at the mill.

His cycle, too, was decorated impressively. It looked like a pony trotting in.

One day, he had entered the mill after drinking arrack and gone about his work. Without thinking he had inserted his left arm into the machine. It wasn't exactly a kamalai bucket, was it, that he could stop the bulls and retrieve it? If anyone asked him, he replied in a normal tone, 'I heard a cracking sound, as if someone was tugging my hand when I was asleep. That was it. One arm was missing. The machine had swallowed it like a bull devouring an ear of sorghum.'

The mill paid him compensation and sent him back to the village. He squandered that money too on drink. His father-in-law, the village headman, remarked, 'The mill owner has given him money in exchange for his arm and asked him to drink. If he hasn't learnt anything after this loss, to whom can we complain?'

That was the way his life had turned out.

Ayya used to drink a lot. After Annan died, he reached a kind of sobriety.

~

This visaakam, it would be five years since Annan died. Each year on the day Aaththa had sat with Aththai in front of the lamp in their house and wept her heart out. While weeping, she would often cry out, 'Where are you, my wise adviser?'

Aththai cried for Janaki too. Ayya kept staring at the bottles hanging on the wall. He sighed often. Mama stood at the entrance, leaning on the door frame.

They made an offering of food in front of the lamp and prayed. No one attended the visaakam festival. All they did was go to the temple and break a coconut in front of the deity.

Ayya had had a lot of respect for Annan. He had consulted him on many matters. Before harvesting the crop in their land, he would always discuss with Annan and decide.

Annan spoke with an adult's maturity. He avoided the company of little boys. He kept himself busy twisting fibre to make rope. He looked after the cattle in Mama's house, wove muzzles for the bulls, a straining lid with moonseed to drain the water from cooked rice. He had learnt a variety of skills. Vadakkuraan had no sense. If he was a real man, he would have faced off with Ayya, who was his match. If he was angry with Ayya, he should have kicked him in the shins. What was he angry about, anyway? It was pointless rage. They hadn't fought face-to-face, had they? Even their small parcel of land should have been handed over to him. He would have been happy then.

What could Annan do about that? Vadakkuraan had killed a boy who was merely grazing goats.

Whenever he thought of Annan, he thought of Vadakkuraan. If he saw anyone grieving at home, he couldn't help remembering Vadakkuraan.

Chidambaram didn't want to herd goats without Annan. For a few weeks, he went along with Karupayya to graze goats. He stopped playing with boys of his own age. Nor did he go too often to the public tank. After tethering the goats at sunset, he would go straight to the temple. He would sit on the compound wall of the temple tank and stare at the ground. His younger sister and the dog would play down below.

Chidambaram took the small sickle that Annan used to carry and sharpened it properly. He couldn't hide it comfortably in his trousers. So he took the dhoti that had belonged to Annan off the washing line and wore it. Two days later, Ayya bought him a couple of two-yard dhotis. If the sickle was hanging from the waist string on his right side, and his dhoti folded up to the knee, it looked normal.

Aththai stared wide-eyed at his dhoti-clad look.

Ayya looked out for any opening to take his revenge. To get information about Vadakkuraan's movements, he befriended a toddy tapper in the area. He anticipated that Vadakkuraan would visit him for his fill of padaneer.

The toddy tapper was a good man. He would never let an indiscreet word slip out of his mouth. He hung his bowls on the palm trees in Vadakkur as well. He would bring down the padaneer before it was daylight. Since dawn was an opportune time, Ayya was hopeful of finishing the job.

Ayya and the toddy tapper would sit together every evening and speak to each other in confidence. They would speak without arousing suspicion.

It was close to dawn on that day when the toddy tapper met Ayya after bringing down the padaneer. He had a large bandage around his left thumb. The thumb was shorter than normal. Ayya asked the toddy tapper about the injury. The toddy tapper replied in a relaxed tone, 'I was holding the curved rim of a pot. The snake lying inside bit my thumb and slithered out. I cut it in two with the sickle and it dropped to the ground. In the same manner, I kept my thumb on a stalk and hacked it off. It was a cobra, after all. If the poison spread, I would lose my life. It was over with the loss of a finger. I've packed the wound with palmyra flowers. It should heal in four or five days.'

Grasping the man's shoulders, Ayya exclaimed, 'Who could be as wise as you, man? You've honed your human mind into a machete.'

From that day on, Ayya grew even fonder of the toddy tapper. Both of them hung about in the palm grove every evening, eating nungu and talking of all kinds of things. Ayya liked to mix tender nungu pulp with the evening's yield of padaneer and drink it.

One day the toddy tapper told Ayya that someone was stealing the padaneer from the palm trees every evening. Ayya was very angry.

'Then we have to find out, right? Find out who the guy is and deal him a couple of hard blows on the back.'

'Why does he have to steal? If he really wants it, he can come to the grove and ask me. I'll give him a little to drink. After all, the money I have today will be with someone else tomorrow. But if he cleans out the yield every evening, how am I to survive?'

'Then you know who is doing it. You have to strike him in the face. Else, you can tell me.'

'Even if I know him, asking him to his face won't be right. I should catch him on the palm tree. But I am wandering all over the fields and groves every day; so, when shall I go and wait for him?'

'Do you have even a little bit of sense? Is it so easy to climb a palm tree? If you are unlucky and drop like a lizard from the tree, that's the end of your life. Will his father come and look after your family then?'

'If he doesn't drink it, can that padaneer come and protect my child? We must pass our days somehow, that's all.'

'Then he will climb all the palm trees and drink all he wants.'

'He is climbing without foot brace or throat cover; that's quite a feat. What'll happen if he slips?'

'You're unfit for this vocation. We have to find a way to fix him.'

'We will, in a couple of days.'

Two days later, the toddy tapper took Ayya to the public tank to see a man who was clutching his stomach in pain. He seemed to be suffering from a bad attack of diarrhoea.

'Since someone was stealing the padaneer, I coated the pot with laxative. It seems this man drank it by accident. Everything that went in is squirting out. If a man comes and asks me directly, I'll give it to him. Why should he climb a palm tree for it? I've been cursed to cling to the trees precariously like a garden lizard because of my past sins.'

The man was doubled over and didn't look up. Ayya also stayed calm. The toddy tapper walked to the nearest palm tree, climbed up and came back with a small bunch of palmyra fruit. He split the outer shell and offered some nungus to the man.

'Eat the pulp along with the skin. Its astringency is good for the stomach.'

Ayya kept staring at the toddy tapper.

Ayya went to the Vadakkur area thrice with the toddy tapper. The toddy tapper would come home at dawn, wake up Ayya and take him along. On all three occasions, Vadakkuraan had eluded Ayya. As usual, it was the fat henchman who had come to buy padaneer. What was the point of killing him?

The toddy tapper had gently persuaded Vadakkuraan to come to the palm grove and drink fresh padaneer at his convenience. But Vadakkuraan was not tempted by that invitation.

Later, Ayya started looking out for Vadakkuraan in the town.

Chidambaram waited a long time for Vadakkuraan. He hung about in the temple ground on every market day, week after week, waiting for the moment Vadakkuraan got down from his carriage.

The sound of Vadakkuraan's carriage was special. The rhythmic tinkling of its bells was redolent of oyil kummi aattam. Bunches of tiny bells were tied around the bull's horns. His henchman always drove very fast. If he raised the whip, its tip would touch the ground in front of the carriage.

Once they arrived in the market, Vadakkuraan would get down majestically from the carriage. He would survey the surroundings with a stately glance. He would straighten the silk towel on his shoulder, hold up his dhoti on one side and walk to the bazaar. The thug would keep fodder for the bullocks and then lie down on the carriage seat.

Vadakkuraan would visit the commission mandis and chat with the owners. Many of the commission mandi owners were his associates, often relatives. He would visit a shop that sold cotton seeds and drink a cup of coffee there.

He would go to the market and hang around for some time. At dusk, he would come to the temple. He would buy coconut and fruits and pray to the deity with those offerings. After his worship, he would enter a restaurant. It was usually dark by the time he started back for his village. He never travelled alone. He always picked up men from Vadakkur who were visiting the market.

On some market days, waiting on the road to Vadakkur did not provide any opportunity. People from Vadakkur travelled on that road constantly in both directions. It would be impossible to kill a man who was sitting inside a carriage. And the henchman driving the cart had to be dealt with too.

Many market days went by in this fashion.

In the market, Ayya would lurk secretly near the spot where Vadakkuraan was standing. Chidambaram had to stay out of Ayya's sight during his excursions. If

Ayya spotted him, he had to invent a different reason for being there and get away quickly.

Killing Vadakkuraan was not going to make Annan come back to life. Why kill him, then – that too, after such a long wait?

What was Vadakkuraan's problem if someone didn't want to sell their land to him? What was that piece of land compared to his vast holdings? Did he imagine that if he took someone's life, the land would become his, or that it would frighten Ayya into giving it up? If he dared, he should have clashed with Ayya face-to-face. He didn't know if Vadakkuraan had ever confronted Ayya and exchanged hot words. Instead, he had vainly nurtured enmity in his heart.

And yet Chidambaram was reminded of Annan whenever he set eyes on Vadakkuraan. It pained him to see Vadakkuraan offering worship at a temple after having taken a young life in cold blood. He thought that allowing such people to walk around freely was wrong. Vadakkuraan was intent on dominating everyone. It didn't matter to him if he killed Annan or anyone else. Someone who thought like that had to be eliminated. It would be a warning to others like him.

People were walking on the mud path between the palm trees. He crouched behind the cover of a bush and watched them till they disappeared, then he went straight to the cane field.

He had to go to the cane field before Ayya returned and prepare a place for them to sleep in. After Ayya came back, they could eat and turn in for the night.

5

From outside the place didn't look like a graveyard. It was one where corpses were both buried and cremated. As with those small flower gardens attached to some temples, a thick cluster of trees, stretching their boughs overhead like a canopy, made it cool inside. As they made their way within, Ayya said, 'See what a cosy spot we've found!'

'Nobody will come here. It's really safe.'

'Never plant trees in a graveyard, they say. But the folks in this village have turned it into a woodland garden.'

'Why not?'

'If there's cool shade, it will make people want to stay on here, they say, attracting plenty of corpses.'

'Then a lot of people would have died in this village, right?'

'Doesn't look like it. Graves are quite sparse here.'

They had to cross a stream to reach the graveyard. There was abundant water in that stream, which flowed into a tank. There was a ridge on the opposite side. It wouldn't be submerged even when the tank was full. They could run along the ridge, climb on to the bank and escape.

From the outside no one could see inside the graveyard. From within the graveyard, however, it was possible to watch people entering from outside. As the day wore on, Chidambaram began to worry about food. They couldn't set up a stove and cook in a graveyard. The smoke from the fire would be visible. Nothing would give them away more quickly. They had no rice left either. The food that Mama had brought had been just enough to feed them last night. As on the previous day, they had to go hungry that afternoon.

Ayya said, 'We can't cook here, son.'

'Never mind.'

'Should we starve to death, then?'

'No one is starving.'

'Of course not. We're eating really well, three times a day.'

'Do you want to eat now?'

146

'Don't you?'

'No.'

Ayya looked at him and then lowered his head.

'If you tell Aaththa, she'll be full of praise.'

'Why?'

'Remember how she would heap food on a plate and call out to you every evening? Aththai would also join her and start looking for you. If I told your mother that you were going without food today, she would be very unhappy. "How could you starve a growing boy?" She would have kicked up a row.'

'I wonder how Aaththa and Thangachi are managing. Are they eating enough?'

'We can't even feed ourselves, and you are talking about them. What's their problem?'

'She must have enough money to buy treats for Thangachi.'

'Yes, she does. Why worry about that when we have our own dinner to deal with?'

'What of it? We will take care of it at one go tonight.'

'We should have some means for that.'

'I'll go to that village and come back. They'll have a coffee stall, surely?'

'You don't have to go. Stay here. I'll go.'

'All right.'

Ayya prepared to set out. Chidambaram got up and moved to the shade.

'Shall I leave, then? Be safe. Don't venture out unnecessarily.'

'Go ahead.'

Walking across the ridge, Ayya climbed on to the bank and left. It didn't look like he was going to visit the neighbouring village. If he was going somewhere else, he probably had some work there.

Yesterday in the cane field, the wet mud had got stuck to his dhoti. He tore off the caked mud. His scalp itched and his eyes were burning. He wanted to bathe to his heart's content in the stream near the graveyard – to swim, dive and simply play around; dive all the way to the floor, stir up the mud and enjoy the water. He also needed to wash his dhoti and shirt.

He hid the sickle and the handmade bombs away from sunlight behind the cover of a jujube plant on the bank. The bombs might explode if they were exposed to the sun. Not likely, though. They were each packed in a cloth wrap to avoid friction. But why invite trouble? Ayya had told him to be careful.

He took the money out of his trouser pocket and stowed it in a knot tied in a corner of the cloth wrapped around the bombs. He had forgotten to ask Ayya if he had any money. Ayya could talk pleasantly if he was in the mood. Otherwise, like today, he was often irritable. Let him manage on his own and come back.

He found a broad stone slab and placed it at the water's edge. He soaked his dhoti and shirt in the stream, and washed them on the slab without making a sound. Then he spread them on the bank to dry.

While swimming in the stream, he found the water warm at first and then increasingly cold. In a few places, the water was deeper than a man's height. He dived deep, climbed back to the surface and looked around. Far away, a few figures were visible on the stone steps leading to the public tank. He swam and played around in the water, making sure that he could rush to the jujube plant at any moment and retrieve his weapons. He filled his mouth with water and gargled loudly, emitting frog-like croaks. He spat out the water like a fountain.

He couldn't bathe like this in the tank in his village. Workers from the match factory regularly washed the chemicals off their bodies in it and the water had a strange smell. One day, a row had broken out over this practice. Sometimes the villagers carried water from the tank for household use. They washed their cattle in it. After the big row, the match factory workers never came near the public tank again.

Aaththa would scold him if he bathed in the public tank. Aththai didn't like it either. She would take him home, make him stand erect and bathe him again. She would wipe him dry with the end of her sari and rub oil on his skin. If his eyes were red, she would look at them and lament, 'All that filth in the water has got into your eyes. They look so bloodshot.'

All said, Aththai was one of a kind.

It was very late by the time he finished bathing in the stream and got out of the water. His eyes were smarting. If Ayya found out, he would be angry.

He walked to the graveyard. Before reaching their hideout, he had to pass a few fresh graves. In one small grave, a stem of pirandai had sprouted leaves. He carried the weapons without getting them wet and deposited them under the mulberry tree. Then he sat leaning against the tree.

The grave they had dug for Annan was equally small. With the legs straight, his body would have been too long for the grave. They folded the legs back before lowering him into the ground. The whole body was not visible because they had covered it with a sheet. His face was disfigured beyond recognition. Because he had lain in the open for four or five days, his body was stinking.

Mama did all the work, bearing his grief with stoicism. Ayya sat like a crazed man, with both hands on his head. Some people had tried to stop Aaththa from coming to the graveyard, but she wouldn't listen to anyone. A picture of grief with her hair loose and dishevelled, she tried to follow them to the grave. In the end, she gathered and tied her hair while muttering something resolutely to herself. Then she stopped crying, beat herself twice on the chest with one hand and went back home. Aththai didn't leave the house at all. She had stretched out in a corner, exhausted from weeping.

People wondered about the incident. Everyone cited a different reason for Annan dying in this way.

'A snake or insect must have bitten him.'

'There's no evidence of that. Why should he lie inside a bush if an insect had bitten him?'

'There was a head wound. Blood was pouring out.'

'He might have tripped and fallen, perhaps?'

'Yes, indeed. Why would anyone trip and fall deep inside a bush?'

Ayya didn't say anything.

Why was Annan's body lying hidden from view – on the sloping bank of the stream, inside a bush at the foot of a white chaste tree – as though his body had been folded and pushed into it?

When the goats reached home on their own that evening, they went looking for him. They searched everywhere for four days. They combed all the fields and groves. He could not be found anywhere. He would never go off leaving the goats behind. There was no place where they hadn't looked for him, no clue they hadn't followed up on. They asked about in the neighbouring villages, but got little more than random statements about how Annan's goats had grazed here and there on that day.

For three days no one at home ate even a morsel. Ayya didn't come home at all. They even tried astrology. The astrologer told them all kinds of things. Relying on his advice, they sent search parties to many villages in the area. A bunch of men came from Chiththi's village to help them out.

On the fifth day, they received information from Vadakkur. It was reported that a corpse was lying curled up behind the cover of a bush. Ayya, Mama and all the others rushed there, fearing the worst. At a bend in the stream, they found Annan's body. As evidence that his body had been dragged and pushed inside, a few twigs in the white chaste bush seemed broken. How did they manage to kill him? He was so careful and vigilant! He wouldn't give anyone a chance to get the better of him. How did he come to such a horrible end, beaten and shoved inside a bush?

Ayya let out a wail.

'Some bastard has murdered my tiger cub and wrapped him in a bundle. They might well have hacked off my right arm.'

No one could find a motive. The old village headman said, 'He wasn't some irresponsible cad caught up in woman trouble, was he? They've broken a sapling and shoved it there. Surely, this is a wanton act.'

The ceremonies were conducted discreetly, without any hubbub in the street. The graveyard rituals were completed without sending word to neighbouring villages.

Chiththi came one day and had a crying spell. She lamented that she wasn't lucky enough to see his body in the end.

Ayya changed completely. Aaththa became thin as a reed. Chidambaram didn't want to graze the goats on the hillside or anywhere else. For how long could he stay idle, without collecting himself?

Annan's mysterious death ruined the peace in their household forever. It's all they could think about. Aaththa and Aththai would sit together for hours without saying a word to each other. No day passed without Ayya and Mama discussing the case. They pursued clue after clue, trying to find out the truth.

Nearly eight months passed. They suspected the cattle broker from Keezhur. Their suspicion was eventually confirmed.

The broker was a ruffian who also mediated in disputes. There was no previous enmity between him and Ayya. If he visited the village, he would talk warmly to Ayya and buy him arrack. If Ayya bought him a drink, he would accept it.

In one dispute, Mama had had a minor clash with the broker. He had spoken to Mama without respect. Mama got angry. He warned the broker that if he ever came to their village, neither of his legs would go back with him. Later, they made peace with each other.

Even then, Mama would not speak to him as freely as he used to. Ayya used to chat with him, though. Aaththa didn't like it. She yelled at Ayya, 'Why do you have to talk to all kinds of riff-raff? Should you trust him just because he is polite to you? Why can't you judge the man's character?'

Ayya did not reply.

When Annan was herding the goats, the broker had picked a quarrel with him. Aaththa used the incident to sow suspicion in their minds: 'It couldn't have happened without his knowledge. Either he did it himself or he knows who did it. He is a poisonous snake. Does he move around in the same way as before? You should watch that first.'

Mama replied evenly, 'All right. We'll look into it.'

Ayya did not suspect him at all.

'How could he, maapillai? The man was buying me arrack till the other day. He wouldn't have dared. I don't think so.'

'No, machaan. He might not have done it in anger, but if somebody had offered him some money, why wouldn't he want it?'

'How could a man be so bold?'

'He did it because he dared. That's how little our lives amount to.'

Ayya grumbled to himself and then fell silent.

He spoke to no one in the street about the broker. The old village headman enquired often. Kaarmegam came by regularly for a chat.

On their street, a few young men got together often to discuss the case among themselves. They had several suspects and would often consult Mama. 'Let's not be in a hurry,' he would tell them. 'We have to investigate thoroughly before coming to any conclusion. Otherwise, an innocent man might get killed.'

Poomani

One weekly market day, Ayya and Mama closed in on the cattle broker on the outskirts of the village. He had some inkling about why they were approaching him. He walked faster and when they started following him, his fears were confirmed.

Dusk was falling. Since no man could see another's face in the fading light, the timing was just right. He turned around and shouted from a distance: 'What's the matter, my brothers? After all this time, you seem to have turned on me. Spare my life. I have children to feed.'

Mama didn't speak. Ayya was furious.

'My son is dead and buried in the ground. Who cares about your children?'

'Please don't talk like that, brother. I'll never betray you.'

'As if you can betray me any further.'

When Ayya moved towards him with his stick raised, the broker ducked and pleaded with him: 'It's not right that you treat me like a suspect. If I'd done anything like that, cut me down right here. I'll only be glad of it.'

'It couldn't have happened without your knowledge.'

'I won't deny that. Yes, it's my fault. I should've told you by now.'

'If you knew, why didn't you tell me?'

156

'You wouldn't keep still, with your hot temper. You'd think I was an accomplice and finish me off. Or you'd go straight to the killer and hack him to pieces. Apart from losing your son, you would've wrecked your whole family. I thought I'd let the situation cool down and then tell your maapillai discreetly. But before that . . .'

'I'll never be consoled, you bastard!'

As Ayya lunged at the man again, Mama shouted at him and got him to back off. Then they took the broker with them and got the whole story out of him. He recounted everything exactly as it had happened.

'I had never imagined that it would turn out this way. I didn't know there was such bitter enmity between you and Vadakkuraan. I didn't know, too, that the goatherd was your boy. It was high noon, and it looked like they were thrashing a boy they'd caught trespassing. There was some stranger standing next to him. I had had a few, you see, so everything was a blur. Since I had drunk a lot on an empty stomach, I wasn't steady on my feet. I couldn't even walk a few steps more and shout at them. All right, I thought, they must be bullying the boy for letting his goats graze on their land, so I went home. The bastard has done this!'

When Aaththa heard about this, she fumed, 'Will he ever come to any good? We should root out his entire family. My womb won't heal otherwise. How can I be a woman if I don't see him bleed? The coward's killed a little boy. Can he face me now? None of you should touch him. I'll take care of him myself on market day. I'll hide a sickle under my sari and cut him down. I'd rather go to jail than grieve about losing my son.'

Mama tried to calm her down.

'Avoid loose talk, 'ma. It'll only bring us shame. His end is fast approaching. Stay calm.'

From then on, Ayya spent all his waking hours brooding about revenge. He talked about it whenever he was drunk. Sometimes he drank just to forget his obsession.

Aaththa would protest, weeping, 'So you crave liquor even at a time like this? Alcohol seems to know no grief.' She would cry inconsolably on seeing Ayya with tears in his eyes.

~

He emerged from the shade of the mulberry tree and checked the surroundings. Then he cut a piece of tender stalk from a young palm tree that had sprouted in a grave. He sat down with it and ran his finger along its edge as if to test the sharpness. Using his sickle, he chopped the stalk into several pieces and fashioned a collection of miniature weapons: hand-knife, spear blade and pole-knife. He shaped them further to make them look beautiful.

If only Annan had carried weapons on the day he was killed, what would have become of Vadakkuraan? His wife and children would be mourning every year on that day. Why did Annan go unarmed, with not even a pole arm?

Couldn't he pick up a stone and throw it? He would have aimed at the man's temple. His aim never missed the target. He tripped and fell, perhaps. That's how they must have caught him.

He was hungry. Ayya wasn't likely to come back any time soon. He must have gone to attend to important business; he would return only when it was over. By the time he returned, it would be late at night. Chidambaram would be famished by then.

If he chewed on something and drank some water, he would be able to withstand the hunger. Going hungry in the afternoon was really hard.

When he was out herding the goats, he would feel dizzy if he didn't eat anything in the afternoon. His face would wilt. If he came home late for his midday meal, Aththai couldn't bear it. She would make it a point to come home and shout at Aaththa.

'Did you look at the child's face? What's he going to earn by grazing goats on an empty stomach? What will happen to him if he doesn't eat on time? Just sell off the goats and keep him at home. What you've earned is quite enough.'

Aaththa would say, 'Who told him not to come home in time for lunch? Or he should take a lunch pail with him. He doesn't do that either. What can I do?'

He didn't like to carry his lunch in a pail. It didn't feel like having a meal at all. As soon as he opened the pail, he would remember mashing and drinking the gruel with Annan and lying down after it under the tree for a nap. If he put a handful of food into his mouth, he would choke with hiccups. No, he didn't like to eat from a lunch pail.

Eating with Annan had been special. Annan would nicely mash the cooked millet into gruel, adding salt and a little water. Then he would add water and salt again. He would drink a little to check the taste. He would scoop some in his hand and check for whole grains. He would be as meticulous as Aaththa preparing a mix of condiments for kuzhambu.

There was a kind of beauty to everything Aaththa did. Her mashing cooked lentil was a sight to behold. Just watching her make kuzhambu, from mashing the lentil to garnishing the gravy at the end, could make anyone feel hungry.

Even the way she cooked millet paste was a sight. Holding the pot with a forked stick wedged on the rim, she would stir the paste with a wooden spatula. With each stroke, the paste would rise from inside the pot and fall away, like someone sticking his tongue out momentarily. The spatula and paste would come together and part instantly, as if playing touch-and-go with each other.

He looked up at the mulberry tree. He saw black fruits hanging here and there on the tree. He needed to climb up. There was no other way to quench his hunger. He climbed the tree slowly and plucked some fruits. He spotted camel spiders wandering up and down the branches.

The fruit was not tasty. Only one or two felt sweet on the tongue. Whenever he saw anyone eat such fruits, he would mock them as shameless gobblers of chicken poop. Whom could he mock now?

After eating a meal of mulberry fruit, he went to the stream, filled his stomach with water and came back. If he still felt hungry, he could pluck some pirandai fruit from the grave in the burial ground and chew it.

He was feeling slightly giddy. If he lay down in the shade, he would fall asleep instantly. But he couldn't afford to sleep. He should avoid falling asleep and stay vigilant. It would be a disgrace if he got caught. His weapons would be of no use. Ayya would feel bad. Mama would scold him.

He wouldn't feel sleepy if he moved about. For how long could he walk around inside a graveyard? At best he could cut palm stalks and make rings and watches out of them. But who would wear them? He needed four or five little boys.

If he gifted a fine, layered ring that he had made himself to Thangachi, she would go everywhere showing it off. If Aththai asked her about it, she would nod her head happily.

'My, my. If she is so proud that her brother has gifted her this leaf ring, a gold ring would make her shun us all! I am an old woman and you are my only hope. I want to give you all my gold jewellery and get a mouthful of gruel in return. Will you give it to me, 'ma?'

It was many years since Aththai stopped wearing gold ornaments. After Janaki's death she wouldn't wear them even on auspicious occasions. No one asked her to. If anyone did, she would break down and cry, and it was never easy for Aaththa to console her.

Aththai was like a small, overripe tomato. Just a light prick with a thorn, and its juice poured out. Everyone spoke pleasantly to her. If anyone said anything to hurt her feelings, she would tear up. Mama was the best person to talk to her. He would talk to her with a smile on his face. If she looked sad, he would tease her.

At home, no one spoke about hurtful matters in Aththai's presence. She couldn't bear it. It was remarkable that she had withstood Janaki's death and Annan's murder.

The evening sun had slanted into the graveyard. Pieces of bone glistened white in a few places. Bullock carts were moving along the road adjoining the neighbouring village. He picked up the sickle and came over to that side to watch the bullock carts. There must be some festival going on in the village. He could hear the sound of anklets worn by the bulls tinkling softly in the distance.

Ayya returned after nightfall. He gave Chidambaram two food packets – curd rice and vadais. Chidambaram opened a packet promptly and started eating.

'Didn't you eat in the afternoon?'

'Yes, I did.'

'Where?'

'Somewhere. I don't remember where.'

'It doesn't look like you ate anything.'

'It's not like you had a big lunch yourself. Fill your belly with what we have now.'

'Did you have enough money?'

'Why, is this food not enough for you?'

'That's not what I meant. Did you have any money to spend?'

'At the eatery where I had gone to buy food, I saw a cattle broker I knew. He is such a talkative fellow. If we met, I wouldn't be able to get away from his chatter. It took me some time to dodge him, go inside and buy the food. I couldn't go looking for another food stall if I wanted to come back early. You were all alone here. Hunh, that's a huge mass of rain clouds in the sky.'

'Do you think it'll rain?'

'Looking at the bank of clouds, yes, it should.'

After eating, they walked separately to the stream to drink water and came back. Then they went to their respective places to lie down for the night.

The sound of drumbeats began to reach them from the neighbouring village. The beat of the pampai was dominant. From the rhythm, he guessed that it must have been for the votive offering of the Pongal feast at a Madasamy temple. That gong-like beat with the cymbals was never played for any other god. They were going to hear it all night till sunrise, it seemed.

If the celebration was close by, he could go and watch. But it would disrupt their sleep. They had to wander quite far the next day. They might fall asleep listening to the steady drumbeats. They had to get up and leave before dawn. Ayya travelled a lot every day. If he was asked about it, Ayya would say, 'Should I ask you to go instead?'

It felt pleasant to lie down on a towel spread on the grass between two plants. It became even more comfortable after he bent back the grass blades in places where they had poked him. If it rained, he mustn't let the handmade bombs get wet.

Ayya lay soundlessly on the other side, behind the cover of a large bush. Ayya had travelled a lot that day. He must be fast asleep.

The drumbeats went on and on. As time passed, they receded into the distance and faded away altogether as he drifted off to sleep.

He awoke with a start at midnight. He could hear the clink of anklets from the far corner; in the distance, the incessant beat of a lone pampai. He hid himself behind a bush. He saw Ayya go out of the graveyard crawling on all fours.

The clink of anklets came closer. Now he also heard the sounds of a hand-bell being shaken vigorously, accompanied by frightening cries of 'aaai!' in between.

He watched intently. It was a man possessed by Madasamy, the deity. After abruptly turning his skullcap around to one side, Madasamy roamed all over the graveyard, picking up pieces of bone. Amid the crunching sounds of someone biting into bone, that 'aaai!' was heard again – and, as he slammed his pike staff forcefully on the ground, the jingle of tiny bells.

The beat of the lone pampai never faltered. The place was lit by a burning torch. When Madasamy finished his graveyard worship and headed back, Chidambaram felt greatly relieved. Luckily, Madasamy hadn't come over to his corner.

The graveyard that Madasamy had to visit was quite far from his temple in the village. It seemed there was no other graveyard nearby. Madasamy was more powerful than any other deity. If the person possessed by Madasamy was weak and thin, he wouldn't survive the frenzied dance. The spirit would simply devour him. Madasamy was a rough deity; and the rituals for the Pongal ceremony were dramatic.

The villagers danced in demonic frenzy for two whole days. That kind of sleepless fervour was not demanded by any other deity. Since they could not endure the exertions every year, they held the festival once in two years.

Chidambaram lay down comfortably as before. Ayya, too, would have come back by now.

In Keezhur, the Pongal festival at the Madasamy temple was held on a grand scale. The two days of the festival were filled with pomp and gaiety. People from seven or eight villages contributed towards the festival by turns and all of them celebrated the festival jointly. During the two days of the festival, all the villagers camped at the temple. The gramophone set for the festival was supplied from his village. He would climb on to the cart along with the gramophone set and sneak away. He had to leave without his mother knowing. Aththai would give him spending money to buy snacks. She would admonish him not to stand in front of the dancing deity.

Those who were to be possessed would sit behind the cover of the banyan tree in the evening and drink as much arrack as they could take in. After that the drumbeat, dancing and shouting were only a kind of preparation for what was to come. Sudalaimaadan, Nondimaadan and Thoondimaadan – one man would dance possessed in the name of each deity.

When Sudalaimaadan danced his way to the graveyard, did his poojai and came back, not even an infant would dare make a sound. The crowd stayed very quiet. As soon as the deity came back, they poured water on his head. Many villagers prostrated themselves before the deity and sought his blessings. The deity declared boons for everyone.

Then food had to be offered to the deity. A pig with a gash across its chest was held face up on a bed of wet sand spread on a platform, and a dish of banana and porikadalai mixed with the pig's blood was kept ready. Once the dish was served, the shouting died down. The deity would eat the whole offering using only its mouth.

They tore open a pregnant she-goat's stomach, removed the kid and laid it in a cradle. A female deity sang lullabies so softly, no one could understand her. They walked the she-goat with the torn belly to the altar. They impaled the kid's neck, suspended it on an iron hook and sacrificed it to Thoondimaadan.

After sunrise, many more goats were sacrificed. Ayya slaughtered the first goat. It was a special honour accorded to him. With a towel tied around his waist and his forehead smeared with sacred ash, Ayya stood with his right foot forward, holding a sickle in his raised hand. The drenched goat shook its head and extended its neck towards the bunch of foliage held in front of its face. Precisely at that moment, Ayya delivered one swift strike at the back of the goat's neck. Cut in two, the headless goat leapt about. Then many others followed Ayya. If the number of goats fell short, then a vow had to be taken for a repeat sacrifice at the next festival. Cock after cock was slaughtered and thrown away. The headless cocks ran around wildly.

About the ritual slaughter of goats, there was some ill-feeling between Ayya and the cattle broker. The broker was angry that Ayya, who was from the neighbouring village, was given the honour of slaughtering the first goat. But when they drank arrack together, everything was forgotten.

After a feast of mutton, a session of villupattu – storytelling through traditional folk songs, to the accompaniment of an archer's bow and string played as a musical instrument – was held. The troupe sang the ballad of Sudalaimaadan. During their singing, Madasamy went dancing over to them, terrorizing the troupe. At once, they had to sing a song devoted to Madasamy:

For your high-stepping legs, ei Sudalaimaadaa,
Drawers made of mulberry flowers, come Sudalai
    dearest!
For your forward-stepping legs, ei Sudalaimaadaa,
Drawers made of madar flowers, come Sudalai
    dearest!

On a bed of wet soil, ei Sudalaimaadaa,
I'll offer you a roasted corpse, come Sudalai dearest!

As the song went on, the deity jumped for joy
and shook his head with pleasure. Finally, he sat
down exhausted. Then the ballad of Sudalaimaadan
continued.

Weak-hearted men could not perform villupattu
at the Madasamy temple. One year, frightened by the
deity's blood-curdling howls, the troupe dismantled
their bow at midnight and fled the village. Similarly,
if the murasu player was new to the game, he wouldn't
be able to withstand the deity's blows.

Nothing could surpass the grandeur of the festival
at the Madasamy temple. In Keezhur the festival was
celebrated last year. It would be held again the next
year.

A drizzle started that was thick enough to disturb
their sleep. Ayya came over to his corner.

'Has the deity left?'

'He left long ago.'

'You were not afraid, were you?'

'Why should I be? I caught on as soon as I heard
the sound of anklet bells. I just hid behind a bush.'

'I slipped out, knowing he would find me if I
stayed here.'

'I saw that.'

'Why are they letting the deity roam this far from the temple?'

'What can they do? Just for the deity's sake, they can't make a graveyard in the village common, can they? So, you won't get any sleep tonight.'

'It looks like this rain, too, won't let us sleep.'

'What do we do if it keeps drizzling?'

'Come. Let's go to the mulberry tree. We can at least shelter there for a while. Carry your weapons without getting them wet.'

Sitting under the mulberry tree kept them dry but the cold spread slowly through their bodies.

'If you're feeling too cold, wrap the towel around your head. Where is it?'

'I've packed the weapons in the towel. I don't feel cold.'

'Seeing how humid it was in the daytime, I was sure it would rain.'

'Did you go far today?'

'Not really. I went looking for a goat trader. He seems to wander around even more than me. I tracked him down finally and made a deal.'

'Are you thinking of selling the goats?'

'We are both on the run. Aaththa is not at home.

Mama is also busy. There is nobody in the village to look after the goats.'

'Are they grazing or lying at home?'

'It seems our common goatherd takes them to pasture. I hear he ties them back himself and locks up the pen. Even then, it wouldn't be like our own man looking after them, would it?'

'They are all kids. If you sell them now, it won't get you a lot of money. Better to wait for some more time.'

'I think so, too. But we are in a really difficult situation. If we surrender, we have to spend a lot on fighting the case. We can't be short of money even to meet emergencies. It won't be right if Mama has to spend on those too. I considered everything before deciding to sell now. What do you think?'

'Do what you think is right.'

'Tomorrow, I plan to show our goats to the trader and settle on a good price.'

'Does the trader know about the case?'

'I didn't tell him.'

'Ask for the goats to be brought outside the village and fix the deal.'

'I have to go there and arrange for it. Mama will scold me.'

'You'll just have to put up with it.'

'Once we surrender, the police may not let us out

on bail. They will quote some random section and keep us inside. It won't be easy to get bail. We have to face these difficulties.'

'Yes. Sure.'

'I wonder what people are saying in our village.'

'What will they say? Don't they know what happened?'

'You think so, son. Not everyone is going to say that killing that man was right. A lot of them would prefer to keep away. Whatever happens in the village, good or bad, most people will think, "Why bother?" and not get involved.'

'They should realize that the troubles we face today could be theirs tomorrow.'

'There is no one who can tell them. If anyone tries, they'll say, "Why don't you mind your own business?" and walk away. From what Mama tells me, it seems everyone will be solidly behind us on this matter. They were united on the day of the killing.'

'Where do we stay tomorrow?'

'Let's not stay in this area. As soon as you get up in the morning, head straight to your chiththi's place. After you pass four or five villages, look out for a bus and get on board. I'll go to our village.'

'Where do we meet, then?'

'I found a place on the way here today. It's a good

location. There is a big banyan tree on the north side. To the east of the tree is a big Ayyanar temple. There is a high compound wall all around it. As a place to stay, it'll suit us perfectly. Today is Friday, right? Stay over in Chiththi's place tomorrow night and come to the temple on Sunday. Whoever gets there first must stay put. All right?'

'Yes.'

Ayya coughed gently. He lit a bidi. The heavy drizzle had deepened the surrounding darkness.

Chidambaram would see his mother tomorrow, carry his sister in his arms. Thangachi might pull a grumpy face, though. He wasn't allowed to spend a single day without seeing her. He had to take her daily to a sweets stall and buy her treats. Once she had her sweets, Aaththa would get some relief. Otherwise, his sister would lie on the floor like a log of wood. Ayya's words would have no effect. His bullying was only meant for other people. If she so much as turned her face away from his, he would be defeated.

'Appaadi. This girl is going to terrorize me. Dei, Chelambaram. Come here and calm down your little sister.'

Sometimes, even if Ayya bought her snacks she would refuse to accept them. They reached her hands through Aththai.

He wondered how Aaththa was managing to take care of his sister. Since they were living in an unfamiliar village, Aaththa might not be able to buy the child whatever she asked for. It was a small village, after all. Aaththa had suffered the most in their family. If he had walked into the police station right after killing Vadakkuraan, she wouldn't have had to leave her home.

The drizzle didn't turn into a downpour. If it had, they would have been forced to look around for a refuge in the darkness. Summer rain never let you off lightly. The wind and the driving rain would lash down with blinding force. At times, a cyclone might also set in.

Ayya kept his head down, as though he was napping.

'You haven't slept well for two days.'

'How do you know I haven't slept?'

'You wake me up every day, don't you?'

'When I wake you up, you don't look like you have slept at all.'

'Oh, I sleep all right.'

'You should sleep well, son. It's not as if our home has been washed away in a flood. If a man doesn't sleep for two days, he will start feeling weak. You need to be alert. What kind of alert? If you hear a sound, you should wake up even if you are fast asleep. That's how vigilant you should be. If you keep awake all night, what will happen to your body? Didn't you get proper sleep?'

'No, no. I did.'

'We have to go through all this trouble just because we killed that bastard. You should have left him to me. But you beat me to it.'

'You weren't sleeping well even when he was alive. I felt bad about that too.'

'What was the use of my keeping awake every night? It all came to nothing. How can I go into the village tomorrow and face our people? "You're all talk and bravado," they'll say, and spit on me.'

'Which fool is going to say that? What great thing have they done, anyway? After all, when their neighbour was being set upon, they tied their dhotis tight around the waist and did nothing.'

'That's right. Who has the right to question me? We are not living off these people, are we? I'll tell them that it was my son who confronted the enemy and finished him off. They knew it was that thug who killed your brother, but no one came forward to support us.'

'Why should anyone fight on our side? They're not really angry, are they?'

'True. But you must feel for your neighbour when something happens to him. That's why we took the lead on so many fronts. Why did they suddenly dismiss so many workers from the ginning factory? Shouldn't we feel angry about it? Even if we suffer today, at least our children won't have a hard life. We must learn to think like that. A man doesn't plant a palm tree to eat the fruit himself, does he? It's like that . . .'

'They will only learn after getting knocked around.'

'Isn't it enough, the knocks they've got so far? That day, in broad daylight, he shot a man down like a sparrow, with policemen standing by. Shouldn't they learn from it? If anyone had stood there instead of that cart driver, he would have met the same fate. If you can learn only from knocks, you'll be kicked around till the end. But they are a lot better now than before. At least no one has said that killing Vadakkuraan was wrong. And all the men turned up with their weapons and stood by us.'

'Yes, they were with us all the way. When I went over from the public tank and saw them, I was amazed. If the men from Vadakkur had come there, I don't know how many bodies would have fallen that night.'

'That's the unity we need. Had we stayed together, we could have butchered that ginning factory owner by now. His weapon is money. When money touches a policeman's lathi, it begins to dance. What do *we* have, after all? If his weapon is inside a bag, we carry ours in our hands. There's no other way out.'

Ayya was getting more and more angry. His speech faltered. The rain didn't let up. Drops of water began to drip from the mulberry leaves.

'They'll wake up now.'

'That's how it seems from what Mama tells me. Let them stay angry. Only then can we take bold steps.'

'It looks like the rain won't stop.'

'Yes. It's pouring down just before sunrise.'

'It will be daylight soon. We can't wait for the rain to stop. Let's go. It won't be wise to leave after sunrise.'

'Setting out is not a problem for me. It's a familiar route. I'll reach there before daylight. I am only worried about you. What will you do if you lose your way in the dark?'

'I know the way. I'll find the road from the sound of trucks, walk alongside below road level and reach the junction. If a bus comes in the meantime, I'll get on board. I know the junction very well.'

'All right, then. Let's go. Collect your things.'

'Go to the village, meet Aththai and tell her to be strong. I wonder how the dog is coping. Ask her to look after it properly.'

'If you come across people, keep walking without getting flustered. If they start a conversation with you, talk normally. If they keep probing, tell them you've come searching for a lost goat. Don't draw your weapons in anger. It'll be a mistake to take them out without proper cause. Keep your things safe when you're travelling by bus. Come to that place I told you about the day after tomorrow. Should I come with you up to the road junction?'

'No. There's no need.'

'Be off, then.'

Ayya started out from the graveyard a little later. Although Chidambaram had difficulty walking on the wet ground under a steady drizzle, it was outweighed by the joy he felt at the prospect of seeing his mother and sister.

6

Chidambaram climbed on to the road and walked under the trees along the edge. When trucks passed, he huddled close to the trees. Some villages were right next to the road and he would then climb down, go around the village and then climb back on to the road.

After some time, the rain stopped and the horizon on the east turned bright with sunlight.

He had already passed seven or eight villages. The road junction was only a short distance away.

Thangachi would have woken up by now. As soon as she got up, she had to be given something to eat. Until that happened, she would cling to Aaththa's legs and follow her around. Aaththa wouldn't be able to get on with her chores. She would say wearily: 'Chelambaram, look here. Our kitty is moaning. Ask her what's wrong.'

He had to wash her face, carry her to the shop and buy her some treats. After that, she kept to herself. If Ayya spotted her, he would say, 'This child has been sitting here all night and munching on something, and none of you have noticed? If you keep like this, child, you will wear out your teeth.'

His sister responded by munching at her sweets even more noisily.

On rainy days, the tower in the middle of the temple tank was a sight to behold. All around it, pigeons would be waiting for the sun to come out. The pigeons cleaned and preened their feathers but they did not, as might be expected, shake them out and take off; instead, they remained glum and immobile waiting for the sunlight. Once the sun reached the temple tower after warming the hillside, the pigeons flapped their wings and flew away. He loved standing on the bank of the public tank and watching the sun rise over the hill.

It was dawn by the time he reached the road junction. He realized that his shirt and dhoti were thoroughly drenched. It became difficult to walk with the sickle hanging inside the wet garment. Sometimes it got stuck to the thigh or dhoti, hampering his stride. If he had to run, he could only do so after removing the sickle.

He untied the cloth in which the bombs were wrapped and pressed them close to his chest. When the wind got stronger, he stopped and held them tight against his side.

He didn't wait for a bus at the road junction. Instead he walked to a pond which was a short distance away and washed his face. He was not sure about boarding a bus. If he walked slowly, his clothes would get dry. It made better sense to walk.

But what would he do if it started raining again? There were no signs of rain. The clouds had fled, and the sky looked clean and bare in the sunlight.

Yet if he travelled by bus, he would see his mother and sister soon. Aaththa would cook a meal for him. He could eat all he wanted and sleep for a long time. Aaththa would watch over him while he slept.

As he thought through both sides of the question, a bus arrived. He tied his dhoti hurriedly and stretched out his hand.

When he reached the village, people were leaving for work. He walked normally, without drawing anyone's attention. He didn't go directly to the village.

There was a coffee stall next to the place where the bus had stopped. He wanted to buy a couple of vadais for his sister but since there was a large crowd of people at the stall, he kept walking.

Chiththi had a small baby. He had not seen it even once. Aaththa said often that the infant was a lovely boy. He wondered where Chinnayya, Chiththi's husband, might be.

He walked along a foot trail. It led away from the village towards the fields. A man and a woman were moving about in a field that had a portia tree at its centre. He stopped and peered intently at them. Yes, they were indeed Chiththi and Chinnayya. Chiththi did not lift her head to look at him.

On reaching the portia tree, he took cover behind it and confirmed their identities once again to himself. Then he stepped into the field. Chinnayya had recognized him from a distance. It appeared that he hadn't told Chiththi yet. She didn't see him until he was right in front of her. When she looked up, she was speechless. Then she laughed and looked at Chinnayya.

'Oh God. The poor boy's had such a hard time getting here.'

Chiththi came close to him and cracked the knuckles of both her hands near his temples to ward off the evil eye. Chinnayya started walking home without saying a word.

Chiththi took Chidambaram aside and sat down with him on the ridge on one side of the main channel.

Groundnut plants had flowered all across the field. Everything was yellow.

She asked him, 'Did you come alone, or has your father come with you?'

'Ayya has gone to our village. I've come alone.'

'You've got nicely drenched in the rain.'

'Just a little. It's all dried now.'

Chiththi tousled his hair and patted it to dry it.

'Hasn't dried at all. If you get soaked like this, what will happen to your health? That wretched bastard. When he was alive, he destroyed your family's peace, and even after he is dead, the family is being torn apart.'

'Aaththa didn't come with you?'

'Why should she come here? She is at home, looking after your sister and baby brother.'

'How is my baby brother? I haven't seen him since he was born.'

Chiththi's eyes welled up.

'He is just fine.'

'Why should you leave him at home and come here? You can look after him and ask Aaththa to work in the field, can't you?'

This was the first of Chiththi's babies to have survived in many years. She had married a long time ago and had had many children, but none had survived. When she was pregnant with this child, Aaththa had come over and helped with the delivery.

Previously, Chiththi would come to their village and deliver her baby in Mama's – her brother's – house. She would spend her days happily nursing the baby. Aththai and Aaththa looked after her very well.

During the period after childbirth, Chidambaram would quietly approach Chiththi and take a pellet of the post-partum medicine from her. The medicine tasted sweet, bitter and sour at the same time. He also got to eat palm sugar as fine as flour. Aththai would pour thick gravy made with anchovies on a plate of rice, top it with a spoon of gingelly oil and give it to him. It had a special taste.

They would send off Chiththi happily every time. A few days later, a messenger would arrive to tell them that her baby had died.

It was Mama who told her not to come this time. Aaththa went over and helped with the delivery. She stayed over for another month and came back. Whenever she was away from home, his sister stayed with Aththai.

Chiththi and her husband bought Aaththa a fine sari. Mama and Aththai came to see the baby. Ayya bought him a baby shirt. Everyone was overjoyed that the baby had survived.

Chinnayya, who had gone home, came back to the field.

'Did you see any of those silly fellows in the village?'

'They've gone out. Why? What will they do?'

'They'll talk some mischief or the other.'

'The way everyone told them off yesterday, they wouldn't dare to talk rubbish again.'

'Come. Let's go.'

When they reached home, his sister was playing by herself. Aaththa was trying to pacify the baby. After keeping his bombs and weapons in a corner of the pyol, Chidambaram came over and picked up his baby brother. His sister came over to him and hugged his legs.

Aaththa was all smiles. She didn't look sad at all. It was her nature. Whatever the sadness, she would keep it locked up in her heart.

Chinnayya was standing at the doorway, watching the street.

Thambi was a beautiful baby. The knit of his brows and those big eyes made him look handsome. To help him to sprout a few teeth, they had tied a brace to his jaw. He tried to bite into anything that was placed on it, accompanied by screeching sounds.

His sister seemed untouched by everything that

was happening around her. Chiththi and Chinnayya wouldn't let her lack for anything. Whenever they visited the village, they always brought her plenty of treats, way more than she could eat.

Chiththi said, 'Your sister stays quiet even when Ayya is not around, but she just can't get by without her Chelambaram. We buy her all kinds of things and attend to her every need. But her face is never lit up like it is today. She must have been thinking of you all these days.'

Aaththa spoke softly. 'How can she stay with her brother all the time? If he has to work, he has to – that's all . . . Has Ayya gone to the village?'

He nodded.

'He went there to meet Mama and consult with the others.'

'What's left to consult with the others, after everything is over? He didn't need to go and discuss something afresh, leaving you all alone.'

'He wanted to come here with me. I said no. How can both of us run around together without attending to the work that has to get done? He went only after Mama sent for him.'

'Who met up with Mama?'

'He had come to see us one day.'

'Is that right? He seems to be all over the place, hardly stays at home. He was here yesterday. Poor Aththai has to stay all alone.'

'That was earlier. I believe she is the one who takes food to Mama in the fields.'

'Has she become that brave?'

Chiththi took the baby from Aaththa.

'The day I left, in the middle of all the tension, she packed a lot of food and gave it to us. I said I had to see you before leaving. Ayya and Mama didn't let me stay. I really didn't want to leave. What could they do to me? Ayya was pressing me to leave quickly. Why did I have to leave? What's so precious about life, anyway?'

'How could we have left like this if you were locked up in the station? We would've come there right away.'

'That's why I agreed to leave. If we get caught, they will abuse us and beat us up. Bastards! Who is there to question them?'

Chinnayya said to him, 'Clean your teeth first, wash up and have something to eat. We'll worry about the rest later.'

Chinnayya went out. Chiththi told Aaththa, 'Hold the baby. I'll get hot water ready for Chelambaram's bath.'

'No. I'll do it myself.'

Aaththa went into the kitchen.

Heat

Chiththi and Chinnayya set out for the fields. Chidambaram looked after his sister and the baby. After finishing her chores, Aaththa bathed him with hot water. She scrubbed away all the dirt from his body. After bathing, he wore one of Chinnayya's dhotis. Aaththa washed his shirt and dhoti. She dried his head with a towel, applied oil in his hair and combed it neatly.

'You've caught a cold from drinking water in all kinds of places. See, your nose is blocked. If you don't apply oil in your hair, your eyes will burn. Did you eat at the proper time? Your father must have dragged you along to all sorts of places.'

While combing his hair, she asked him to tell her everything that had happened to them. He didn't tell her about the food problem. She would have been very unhappy if he had told her.

After drinking some gruel, he started out for the field. His sister came along with him. In the field, he did weeding work until midday. Everyone was back home by noon. They ate together. Aaththa remembered Ayya.

'Don't know where he might be right now. He is never bothered about food. Did he say he was coming here?'

'No, he isn't. We are planning to meet tomorrow.'

'Poor boy, you have to run around so much.'

The oil bath followed by a hearty meal had made him feel drowsy.

'I'm feeling sleepy. Let me lie down some place outside and come back.'

Aaththa wouldn't allow it. 'Why do you have to go out? Just sleep here on the pyol. We'll keep an eye out. Who is going to come here? Your chinnayya will look out for you.'

'He doesn't seem to stay here much. Where has he gone?'

Chiththi said, 'He must have gone to the trunk road. He will hang about there, watching for new arrivals. See, a couple of policemen found out somehow and came to the village the day before yesterday.'

'Did they come here too?'

Aaththa said, 'It was evening. I was feeding your sister. Chinnayya rushed in. He explained the situation to me, then he took me along and left me in the chakkili cheri.'[8]

'They must have asked tough questions.'

'When they asked Chinnayya about the murder, he said, "Is that so? We came to know only after you told us," and sent them away.'

---

[8] cobblers' street

'How did he come to know about them?'

'When they got down from the bus, they enquired at the coffee stall, asking for Chinnayya. He saw them.'

'And he figured that they were policemen?'

'That close crop above the nape of the neck gave them away, he says.'

'A good marker. Did no one here tell them anything?'

'If some people clam up, there are others who will talk, right? Are all five fingers the same? A couple of men didn't like my staying here. They said, "Why risk trouble over a problem in some other village?" Chinnayya told them, "If there's trouble, I'll handle it myself. I don't need you to come with me." After that, the villagers got together and discussed it – everyone is of the same mind now.'

'When there are such men in our own village, how can we fault others?'

Sitting in the doorway, Chiththi was sorting and picking stones from a pile of green gram in a winnowing pan. She kept glancing down the street.

Chidambaram was feeling drowsy. He spread a mat, kept the weapons next to it and lay down to sleep.

A lot of people gathered in the house that night. Women peeped in, as if gawking at a spectacle.

Aaththa and Chiththi answered their queries patiently and sent them away.

An old man sat next to Chidambaram on the pyol. There were four or five important men of the village sitting along the edge. They were chatting about all kinds of things among themselves. He remained silent.

'All said, the boy is really brave. Who will dare kill a man in the middle of a street, in front of so many people?'

'How can you say that? When your own brother is murdered in cold blood, how can you keep quiet and do nothing? Still, it does take a stout heart to do such a thing at his age.'

'True. In those days, we were nervous about going to work with a sickle wedged behind our arse. We were scared that the sickle might cut us and make a mess.'

'It's the scared man who'll get injured first.'

The old man's face lit up suddenly.

'That's right. One day we were carrying bundles of paddy sheaves. We had to carry them across the stream and reach the threshing floor. The stream had a little water flowing. There was this one boy who had wedged a sickle in his waist string, behind the loincloth. If he had carried his load without worrying the sickle, it would have stayed in place. With a bundle on his head, this fellow kept touching and checking the sickle with every step. Finally, while we were going down to the stream, the sickle slipped downward. He clutched at it with one hand to keep it from slipping further. With that, he was unable to balance the load on his head, and he fell down. The sickle cut into the flesh of his buttocks, giving him a double arse!'

'He was lucky that it did no worse.'

'How can a man who is scared of a sickle hold a billhook? There is a right technique for each weapon. Look at this boy here. Who taught him anything? Yet he has killed a man.'

'Any other boy would've been caught by now.'

'Still, the police might arrest him and take him away.'

'Policemen don't have any other work. They keep going from village to village.'

'They came to our village too, didn't they?'

'I have a question. Why are they so charged up? They're coming after this boy with full force. It's not as if he has killed their father or uncle.'

'If a man kills someone for committing a crime, the police should let it be and stay away.'

'If they help a criminal, wouldn't it encourage others like him?'

'This is a bad time for good people.'

'One day is not like another, is it? If some wicked fellow kills a policeman on a bad day, what will they do then? His family will be on the streets.'

'Where will it end, finally? It will turn into a fight between this boy and the police.'

'Who thinks about all that?'

'If a fellow can't even think, why does he go to work in a police station?'

'Even if he can think, they'll blunt his brain when he starts working.'

'Not everyone is alike, right? Inflamed by hatred, a man might think, "Anyway I am going to jail; let me finish off another guy before that."'

'Who is worried about jail? It means nothing to a man who doesn't want to live any more. Do they think they can frighten people with jail? If Annan goes to jail, his thambi will finish off one more fellow. It's like taking hot embers and tying them in a bundle at your waist.'

'How long will they keep this boy in jail? When he comes out as a young man, he is going to kill another guy.'

'We'll find out when they present evidence, conclude the case and put him in jail.'

The old man began to chat with Chidambaram.

'Has your father gone to your village?'

'Why do you ask?'

'Just like that. You've come alone, haven't you? Where has he gone, leaving you alone?'

'How can he travel with me all the time? He has a lot of work to do.'

'That's right. It's not advisable for everyone to roam together. Your uncle is a clever man. He will have a solution for everything.'

'I think Ayya will meet him and talk things over.'

'What's there to discuss? There is nothing to worry about. It had to happen. You shouldn't back off now. You have to fight the case, even if it means selling everything you own. It will be a shame if the people in your village don't stand by you.'

'Sure they'll stand by us. It's not as if we've robbed anyone.'

'You said it.'

The rest of them were talking among themselves in small groups. Chinnayya did not budge from the entrance. Holding Thangachi against her shoulder, Aaththa was gently patting her back.

The old man said generally, 'Adei, I heard that some fellow in our village had complained about this. Who is that son of a zameendar, da? If we are attacked tomorrow, where will you go for shelter? Whatever is their lot today could be ours tomorrow. Think about it. If you continue to blabber, I'll give you a hiding. Watch out.'

'Nobody is complaining.'

'I am glad to hear that.'

With a steady flow of visitors throughout the day, it got very late. Aaththa talked patiently to the women before seeing them off.

His sister had fallen asleep before the night's meal. After setting her down in the terrace block, Aaththa came back and served food to everyone.

He asked Chinnayya, 'Why don't I go and sleep in the field?'

'What an idea! Do you think that this fellow here is not a man? Just spread your mat on the pyol and go to sleep. Remember, someone can lay a hand on you only after they've dealt with your chinnayya.'

'I didn't mean it that way. I want to be careful, that's all.'

'Of course we are being careful. If you stand at the far end of the pyol, with one leap you can climb on to the eaves and jump out. For this you want to leave the house, is it? Madhini,[9] look at the way our Chelambaram is talking!'

Aaththa said gently, 'Living here, I am already a

---

[9] sister-in-law, especially elder brother's wife

burden to you. Why should he come here and create more trouble? That's what he is saying.'

'Is that so, Chelambaram?'

'Why should I drag everyone into trouble, Chinnayya?'

'This is atrocity, not trouble.'

Chiththi told Aaththa, 'When I delivered this child, you came over and stayed here for months. Weren't we a burden then? And before this, I came to you for so many deliveries. You used to wash everything including my sari and bathe me with hot water without wincing even once. Was I not a burden then?'

'Go on, you! As if I've done something great and saved your life. Go and attend to your work. Chelambaram won't go anywhere. You can sleep on the pyol, son.'

Aaththa fetched a mat and spread it on the pyol. Chiththi was sleeping next to her baby in the terrace block. After leaving the front door slightly ajar, Chinnayya stretched out on the floor with his head next to the doorstep.

Aaththa stroked her son's scalp to pick lice from his hair.

'If you are always on the move like this, it's bad for your health. Even a grown man will fall ill if he drinks water from a different place every day. His throat will dry up. What does your father say?'

'What will he say? We shouldn't be on the run. He wants us to surrender in court.'

'How can you present yourself suddenly, without finding a way out?'

'He'll discuss it with Mama.'

'You have to surrender if Mama asks you to.'

'I somehow feel that we shouldn't.'

'Why do you say that?'

'We should have boldly surrendered to the police immediately after the killing. If we escaped and went on the run instead, we should wander around forever. We must test their courage with ours. To go to them and say, "Here we are, take us in," doesn't seem right at all.'

'For how long can we keep you running?'

'Well, there are two more left. I should finish them off too and surrender.'

'The man who has wrecked someone's family is not going to get away, is he? That brute killed one of ours, and now he is dead. Like him, the other one too will meet his fate.'

'I am only worried about you and Thangachi living away from home. Otherwise, I would just take off without telling Ayya.'

'And all of us should live without seeing you, is it? How will you dare tell your sister?'

Aaththa had lost her courage.

'If I went to jail, would you see a lot of me?'

'We'll be relieved that you are staying put in one place. We'll see you now and then.'

'Then our family will be at peace again?'

'Our peace was ruined a long time ago. We lost everything in life the day we lost our fine boy. We've avenged that murder. I feel relieved now, relieved that I have a son who could do it.'

'When I think of everything, I feel we should surrender.'

'Anyway, Ayya will come back with a decision.'

Aaththa remained deep in thought.

'If we surrender to the police, will you go back to the village?'

'After I go there, who will dare come after me? The fellow who does will have to deal with me.'

'Poor Aththai has no company.'

'That's what I am worried about. Even on good days, she is not very strong. With no one around, she will just crumble and collapse. How will Mama cope with everything by himself?'

'I would really like to see Aththai.'

'I want to see her even more badly than you.'

'We must tell them to bring her sometime.'

'She will come running, won't she?'

'Or I should go and see her.'

'Not a good idea, son.'

'Thangachi is whimpering. Go and sleep, Aaththa. Wake me up well before sunrise. I must leave before there is enough light for people to recognize me.'

When Aaththa got up, he heard Chinnayya's voice, 'Do what your mother says, Chelambaram. Don't spoil our sleep.'

Chinnayya had been listening to everything they said to each other.

'Haven't you gone to sleep yet, Chinnayya?'

'I can sleep any time. What about it?'

Chidambaram fell silent. As thoughts crowded his mind, sleep seemed to recede further away.

Whatever be the decision Ayya came back with, whatever be the situation in their village, and regardless of whatever may happen in the future, Aaththa must not stay on here. She had to return to their village. His sister would get better only in Aththai's good hands. If he surrendered to the authorities, he wouldn't be able to look after his mother and sister. If Aththai and Aaththa had each other for support, it would give them strength. Mama would look after them. The family would run smoothly.

When Ayya returned, Chidambaram had to make it clear to him. Ayya was usually in his own world, talking about all kinds of things. He didn't think a whole lot about family matters. If he spoke his mind once, that was it. If asked again, he would say, 'Should each of us carry the rest on our shoulders? Why are we given hands and legs – for nothing?'

In any event, going to jail voluntarily was not a good move. Why should he go to jail? If killing someone meant going to prison, then the ginning factory owner should have gone first. Vadakkuraan should have followed him. If Chidambaram alone was punished for his crime, how did that make sense? Maybe they had to make sure that the jails were always full. Like child snatchers, policemen would be roaming the streets to catch the next fellow and file a case. Sometimes they would wake up a beggar and take him to the station. Under suspicion, it seemed. It was ridiculous.

At the same time, sale of arrack would go on briskly inside the roadside stall. The policemen would be chatting intimately with the shop owner. Even the old woman passing by could tell them who the criminals were. The old village headman said often, 'Tell them to go away. These are people who let the shitter get away and wrestle with the turds.'

The first crowing of a cock that morning could be heard vaguely. He had fallen asleep. Someone tapped him awake. He got up. Ayya was standing before him.

What a surprise. He had gone to their village, and he was back the same night: a really difficult journey.

'Have you been here for a while? I nodded off to sleep.'

'I came just now.'

'So, you had to walk all the way here.'

'You've seen your mother and sister, haven't you? How is our bouncy little boy?'

Aaththa and Chiththi came out and stood near the pyol. Chinnayya was sitting near the entrance.

In the terrace block, black smoke from the kerosene lamp fluttered like a sari hung out to dry in the wind. The baby lay on the floor watching the smoke draw a sketch on the wall and move on. Thangachi was fast asleep.

Chidambaram got up, washed his face and shook off the drowsiness from his body. He picked up the sickle and tucked it into his waist string, and secured the handmade bombs.

'Shall we leave?' said Ayya.

'This is the right time. We can pass before people can see our faces.'

He visited the terrace block to have a glimpse of

his sister and baby brother. As he was leaving, he told Chinnayya, 'Take Aaththa and Thangachi to our village and leave them there.'

'No, no. They have to go alone,' Chinnayya joked.

Ayya looked at Chiththi.

'Don't leave the little one on the floor with the kerosene lamp so near, 'ma. The way he bounces around, he may topple it. Accidents can happen. And you've suffered a lot because of children.'

Both of them set out from the house. Asking Chiththi to stay back, Aaththa came along with Chinnayya to see them off. When they climbed down to the cart track behind the house, Chinnayya said, 'Should I come with you?'

'As if our wandering around is not enough. Go home.'

Ayya started walking. Aaththa caught up with Ayya in two quick steps.

'Go if you have to. But don't starve my boy. It might stress him.'

'Who, your boy? With the kind of determination he has, he is going to make *me* feel stressed.'

'Aaththa, take good care of Thangachi,' he told his mother at the last moment and walked away.

7

'It's seven days now. How the days and hours have flown!'

Ayya walked in step with Chidambaram. The day had erupted like a massive blaze. The vigour in their stride during the cool hours of dawn had evaporated in the scorching heat. They trudged on, carefully avoiding the foot trails.

'A week from now, they'll offer food to Vadakkuraan's soul.'

'Who will perform the ceremonies?'

'That ginning factory owner is around, isn't he?'

'Oh yes. He'll do it.'

'How many children did Vadakkuraan have?'

'Who knows what goes on in that fellow's house? There's a small boy who goes to school. And a daughter, I think. He got her married.'

'Local boy?'

'No. From a village in the east.'

Ayya untied his mundasu. The sun had spread to the fields. It had begun to suck the moisture from the air. The wild plants that had once looked sprightly in the shade wilted under the sun and gradually lost their natural splendour. They walked past lands left fallow.

'It looks like we may not find water even to wet our tongues.'

'That's right. Yesterday's rain seems to have skipped these parts.'

'Even if it rains heavily, the water won't stay on the ground. That's the kind of terrain here. I see a village ahead. Let's see if we can find water over there.'

'We shouldn't enter the village. We can get some water if there's a well on the outskirts.'

'There *has* to be one.'

As they walked around the village, they saw women moving about in a dried-up stream. The women were fetching water from a freshwater spring in the middle of the stream. They couldn't approach the women and ask for water; it wouldn't be proper.

Ayya looked at him. 'Are you thirsty?'

'I ate just now. How can I feel thirsty? If I can wet my tongue and wash my face, it'll help me walk longer.'

'Yes, it will give us strength.'

'That's just what I said. Never mind if we can't get it in this village. We'll drink some on the way, wherever we can find it.'

'We'll find it difficult to walk if we are parched.'

'What can we do? We can't go and beg before so many women.'

'I think so, too. Else, we can dig for a spring.'

'We can't do that. All the women from this village seem to be standing by that stream.'

'Can't you see – it's their only source of drinking water.'

'If it rains heavily and floods close up the spring, what will they do?'

'They'll drink the water from the local tank.'

'What a fine village. They have to scrounge daily just to get some drinking water.'

'These people at least have a source nearby. Some villages don't even have that. They go from village to village to fetch water, like pilgrims trekking to some temple pond to bring back holy water.'

'We'll surely find a well in the next village. Let's move on before the women see us.'

The next village was some distance away. On the way, they found a small wood of wild thorn trees. How had the villagers allowed so many trees to survive? In any other village, they would have dug up everything, burnt it for charcoal and made a lot of money.

They saw a large pile of gravel and broken stones like a hillock in front of them. The well must have been dug really deep. There were standing crops in the fields all around. Tomato plants had grown and spread across a small patch adjoining the pile of gravel stones. At the bottom of every plant, as if hatched by a brood of hens, there were ripe tomatoes.

Ayya asked him, 'Why don't you pluck a couple and chew on them? It will quench your thirst.'

'Poor man. He must have worked so hard to draw water for his plants. Should we hit him in the belly? If there's water in the well, we'll drink it. If there's none, we'll move on.'

They peeped into the well, straining their necks as they tried to spot the water.

'What a man! Look how deep he has dug.'

'No use feeling unnerved. You have to dig one, selling all your assets if you have to, if you want your family to survive. You need to fill your belly first. Profit and the rest can come later.'

'Why should anyone work so hard?'

'It *is* hard work, but idling won't fill your belly, right? Why are we wandering around like this? If we had given our land to Vadakkuraan, we wouldn't be facing all this trouble. He was angry that our land didn't go to him. We had to sign it over to him like the others had done and work as coolies – or take to stealing.'

'What was his problem if we kept our land?'

'That's what you're saying, son. But he didn't see it that way. He had built a farm by snatching land from so many people. He wanted to rule over all that land. Greed for property never leaves a man. It won't fade away even if he is cut to pieces.'

Ayya's expression had changed. Chidambaram looked at Ayya. 'We can't climb down this well. I don't see any steps.'

'Is it really a well? A bull will drop dung before it brings up two buckets of water here. Even if you feed the animal a bundle of seedling waste daily, it still won't be enough. Let's move on.'

Ayya laughed.

Chidambaram's thirst had become more acute by the time they reached the next well. It was a lone well in the middle of rain-fed lands and so the surrounding fields were parched; even the green of the vegetation looked pale.

When he looked into the well, he was overjoyed.

'There are steps here.'

'The owner must be a good man.'

Ayya stood waiting in the kamalai pit. Chidambaram hurriedly got into the well, drank water and washed his face. Ayya said, 'Don't bathe here. We'll find some other place by noon. Come up fast.'

Next, Ayya quenched his thirst.

Instead of wading through the watered patches in the fields, they walked on the ridges flanking the main channel. A variety of crops were being raised there. The owner must be a shrewd fellow. He was growing both cash crops and food grains in small patches, with a larger area under cash crops. In the surrounding area, sorghum seedlings had been planted densely to yield fodder for his cattle. The saplings appeared fresh and green.

Ayya looked closely at the patch and said, 'See what he has grown between the seedlings.'

'What can you sow in a field like this? This must be some wild plant.'

'They are cannabis plants. Our fellow is clever. No one will suspect him. This is the perfect spot for growing cannabis.'

'Why would he do this?'

'When farmers start doing business and making a pile of money, they stop thinking. They'll do anything for money. If he packs this plant and sends it out, from root to fruit it's all cash. Even if he sows two acres of millet, he won't make as much money.'

'So much demand, eh?'

'What do you think? Even policemen buy a packet of this powder, strip a cigarette, and stuff it with this powder. With that kind of demand, farmers may as well grow this crop.'

Chidambaram asked hesitantly, 'Can we reach by noon?'

'If we step up our pace, we will. My stomach is griping, but here we are, talking about other people's lore.'

'We drank some water just now, didn't we?'

'Oh yes. We've drunk so much water that we can go without food for two days. But if we stop to pee somewhere along the way, we'll die of hunger.'

'Food won't come on its own. We must go and find it.'

'We are forced to wander daily in this wilderness. What sort of life is this? A dead man's life! And your mother has set me a big task: don't starve Chelambaram. The woman should have cooked and packed something for us.'

'She's taken refuge in that house, and you want her to make something for you? It's a lot of trouble for poor Chiththi.'

'Too true, given their situation.'

'Come with me, then. We'll get there and think about the rest.'

'I am wondering if I should come with you even that far.'

'Why? Do you have to go somewhere?'

'I have to, don't I? I have to collect the sale amount of our goats from the trader. There will be a lot of expenses in the coming days. I also want to give your mother some money.'

'Where will you see Aaththa tomorrow?'

'She will come to us. I'll tell you about it later. I have to collect the money first. I must track him down and grab it from him. He won't give it easily. He'll make some excuse or the other, and slip away like an eel.'

'You go ahead, then. I'll carry on by myself.'

'See that banyan tree over there? You can go there directly from here. At noontime, get yourself a snack from one of the villages nearby. I might suck the life out of you by the time you get to jail. Mama's going to tell me that we are in this trouble only because we did something beyond our capacity instead of staying quietly at home. That we are roaming around half-starved as a consequence means nothing to him.'

'Don't you have a stomach too, like the rest of us?'

'Oh yes, I do. Without one, how could I wander around for so long, eating and shitting regularly?'

'Are you going to leave now or not?'

'I am leaving. I'll be back before it gets dark. Let's go into the temple after I am back. Stay outside until then.'

'Why?'

'Nothing in particular. I don't want you to go alone into the temple. We have to be careful. Anyway, do whatever you want.'

Ayya walked away. Chidambaram noticed how tired he seemed suddenly.

He ran to Ayya and said, 'I have a little money with me. Do you want to carry some for your expenses?'

'What am I going to spend on?'

'Keep it for anything that might come up.'

'No, no. Let it be with you. I won't come back without collecting our money.'

Ayya walked away briskly.

Though Chidambaram was aiming for the banyan tree, he couldn't go there by the direct route. He took a longer path. Outside the villages, people were at work in the fields. He walked steadily, making sure he didn't arouse any suspicion. As he walked on, he came across more fields under cultivation. In a few wells, they were drawing water with a kamalai bucket.

A pump set juddered. He cooled his feet by dipping them in a canal. He soaked his towel in the water, wrung it to get rid of the excess water and wrapped it around his head.

Hunger gnawed at his stomach. He had to put something in his belly before noon, or he would feel giddy. He didn't know when Ayya would return. Ayya would bring some food with him.

Ayya might wake him up in the dead of night as he had yesterday.

There was no way he could reach the temple in time and cook a meal. He would have to collect the necessary materials. That was impossible. So he had to enter a village on the way and buy porikadalai along with palm sugar for his lunch. He should be vigilant while entering the village. If anyone started a conversation, he should reply discreetly. Moving away from the cart track, he walked along a ridge adjoining some fields. In one field, sweet potato had been harvested and the upturned soil left to settle. In several places, the tubers that had been missed during harvesting had started sprouting leaves. It appeared that the farmer hadn't ploughed the soil after harvesting and picked all the missed tubers.

Because there were cropped fields all around it, pigs couldn't reach there. If pigs had entered that field, they would have dug them out. For little boys who didn't know how to pluck a tuber, the pigs' jostling was a source of joy. First, they wore out their fingernails from endlessly scratching the soil in search of tubers. Unable to dig with their nails any more, they followed the pig. They waited while the pig toiled hard, and when it was about to get the tuber out, the boys chased the pig away, grabbed the tuber and ate it. If after a lot of pushing and shoving the pig went quiet, it meant that the pig had spotted a tuber. That was the sign for the boys to move in. Some pigs did not let the boys come near. They grunted fiercely and chased the boys away. The boys' scampering away was quite a sight.

A tuber with a tender shoot tasted very sweet.

He fetched a dried-up twig and whittled one end to a sharp point using his sickle. He scratched the ground with it in a lot of places. The twig was handy for digging into the soil. He was able to dig out tubers quickly. Most of them were sand-coloured tubers.

He hadn't expected to collect so many. He wiped away the dirt on the tubers and tied them in a bundle with his towel. If he ate all the tubers raw on an empty stomach, he would get a stomach ache. He peeled off the skin from one sweet potato and chewed on it as he walked. The sweet juice from the tuber went down the gullet and cooled his stomach.

There was a village ahead. Once he crossed it, the banyan tree would be very near. He hid the bundle of tubers inside a thicket of plants and walked into the village. Since it was noon, there weren't many people about. He asked an old man for directions to a shop. He walked to the shop and bought a box of matches, a small quantity of palm sugar and a cake of soap. No one questioned him.

When he climbed the bank of the irrigation tank, and stood finally in the shade of the banyan tree, he felt as though steam was rising from the crown of his head.

In many places the aerial roots of the tree were embedded in the ground like elephant's feet. The age-old banyan tree had spread a canopy over the curving, wide bank of the irrigation tank.

Adjoining the western bank was the compound wall of the Ayyanar temple, as tall as a man. The temple was quite small. There was a lone deity inside a cement structure while several others stood in the open compound. Bigger than all of them was a large horse with its forelegs raised and mouth agape. There was an opening in its underbelly that was large enough for a man to enter. He wondered how they had managed to build it with brick and mortar to look like a real horse.

Set in the front section of the compound wall was

an even bigger gate. The iron gate across the entrance was locked. The deities were dressed in new costumes. A festival must have been held here recently.

In front of the temple, there were plenty of charred remains from the fires on which pongal had been cooked for offering to the deity. The temple must be common to all the surrounding villages.

One way to enter the temple was to climb on to the roof of the temple from the western bank and jump down from the compound wall. Or you could climb the outer wall, using the gaps in the stone wall as footholds. But he would be clearly visible from outside: people would become suspicious. The best way to enter was from the bank. He could casually climb on to the roof while walking by, unnoticed by anyone.

The irrigation tank was full. People never visited the temple side of the tank. And so he couldn't find even a small pot. In a pit nearby, the curving rim of a broken pot was visible in the dirt. He dug it out gently and washed it in the tank. He could salvage one half of the pot. If he kept it slightly tilted, it could hold a fair quantity of water.

He washed the sweet potatoes and put them in the broken pot, fetched water in it and kept the pot on an old stove that he augmented with a few stones. Now his hunger didn't feel so acute.

While the sweet potatoes were cooking, he dug a small pit near the stove, gathered some round pebbles and played a game like marbles against himself. When he remembered the bombs tied around his waist, he dropped the pebbles. After keeping the bombs along with the sickle safely inside a hole at the base of the banyan tree, he found a couple of sticks and played kitti. He played both sides of the game – hit from one end, field and toss from the other. He imagined that his brother was hitting and he was picking up the kitti.

Annan was an ace in playing kitti. No one could make him field and toss. He would become the hitter in just one turn, while the others would be left to field and toss the stick to him. This is why no one wanted to play with Annan. But Chidambaram would provoke Annan and challenge him. 'If you think you are such a big shot, come for one game today. See if I don't make you pick and toss till you are begging to be let off.'

Annan wouldn't get angry. He would merely groan with a gentle smile playing on his lips. 'Look at the guy who is going to make me pick and toss. Go away quietly and do your work.'

'You'll know when you come to play. See how he talks, farting because he is afraid of facing a little boy!'

Aaththa would do her chores while keeping an eye on them.

'Aaththa, did you see that? Annan can't come to play kitti with me.'

Aaththa would say teasingly, 'Dei, will you lose to this kid?'

'Forget losing. If you come to play with me, I will make you pick and toss even if you're crying. Do you agree?'

'What do you say now, Chelambaram?'

'Why does he talk so much? He'll find out when he comes to play.'

When both of them went to play, Annan would as always win. After wearing him out, Annan would say, 'Chelambaram, you come and hit. I'll pick and toss for you.'

'See if I don't collect a very good kitti and stick tomorrow, become the hitter and make you run around!'

'Come, let's go home today. Tomorrow, you can pick up a nice stick from the hillside.'

While they were eating at night, Aaththa would say, 'What now, Chelambaram? Your brother looks a bit out of sorts. Did you make him pick and toss today?'

'This stick doesn't hit well, Aaththa.'

'That's why I asked you. Don't you need to find a

good stick? So you lost today, did you? Then you must have run around a lot. Have some more rice. You'll be able to win only if you eat well.'

Even then, Annan would be eating with a smile on his face. Chelambaram's wish to beat Annan at least once was never fulfilled.

By the time he finished playing under the banyan tree, the water on the stove had shrunk; the sweet potatoes had cooked nicely and split open. He poked one with a stick. It wasn't raw. He doused the stove, took the pot down and tilted it till all the water was drained. The smell of sweet potato was wonderful. He took out three or four, broke them into pieces and spread them on the banyan roots to cool. Along with a half block of palm sugar, he gobbled up the still-hot potatoes. After drinking water from the irrigation tank at the end of the meal, he let out a big belch.

Now he would not feel hungry at all. He could even go without food that night. It would do if he ate his next meal tomorrow. When Ayya returned, he could eat the remaining sweet potatoes.

After keeping his weapons on the slope of the bank, he washed his shirt and dhoti with soap and spread them out to dry. He made sure that water did not splash on the weapons. Even while he was carefully applying soap on his clothes, he kept an eye on the weapons.

Ayya would say, 'A king cobra spits out a gemstone and hunts prey by its light. As soon as it smells a human, the cobra rushes to the gemstone and swallows it. So vigilant. If it loses the gemstone, it will die. We should guard our weapons the same way.'

He picked up and wore the dried clothes, and went for a short walk. There were a lot of barren plots around. Kurandi had flowered abundantly in the red soil. He plucked as many flowers as he wanted and put them on his towel.

His sister loved kurandi flowers. He picked them for her whenever he took the goats for grazing. Then he got hold of a thread and, sitting in the shade of a palm tree, wove a foot-long string of flowers. When he gave it to his sister, she wore it proudly in her hair. No matter how many chores were pending, Aaththa was not allowed to budge without adorning Thangachi's hair with flowers. Else, she went crying to Aththai, who had to do it. Everyone had to tell her that she looked beautiful with flowers in her hair. Until that happened she never left anyone alone. If Mama was not at home, she wouldn't sleep till he got back. If he was really late, she would fall asleep holding the flowers in her hands.

He picked up a plantain fibre lying on the ground near the temple, wet it with water and wove the kurandi flowers together into a big garland. He took the garland and tied it around the neck of the horse inside the temple. It was beautiful to look at. As the garland swayed in the breeze, it looked as if the horse was galloping. He was thrilled at the sight.

He spread a towel on the temple's terrace and stretched out on it. He watched the ever smaller ripples rise and fade in the watery expanse of the irrigation tank. When Aaththa ground coconut pulp on a flatbed mortar, it looked like this.

Above the temple, a couple of aerial roots were hanging within hand's reach. He soaked some plantain fibres in the water and bound the roots together. Then he collected a few sticks and fashioned them into a hammock resting on the aerial roots. He also picked up the tattered palm-leaf mats lying on the terrace and spread them on the hammock. He climbed on to the hammock and tried to swing. It worked perfectly. Since the hammock was quite wide, he was also able to lie down along the edge and swing back and forth. When he lay down, the sky stretched above him as if he was astride a flying horse.

As the sun slowly set, the screeching of parrots in the banyan tree rose to a crescendo. There must be plenty of parrot nests in the tree holes. If he climbed up, he could catch a lot of hatchlings. He could nurture them as pets.

Catching the little birds in the holes was dangerous. Snakes that came to hunt mice and squirrels lurked in the holes. Once a boy from a neighbouring village had put his hand inside a hollow, thinking it was a parrot's nest. At the first bite, he thought it was a hatchling. 'Oh, you are pecking at me,' he laughed and put his hand in again. There was a second bite, and that was it. He dropped down like a wood lizard. When the adults inserted a sharp pole into the hole, they speared and pulled out a big cobra.

At dusk, the din of weaver birds was unbearable. He got down, walked to the bank, squatted down to shit and came back. Luckily, no one came to the temple to light lamps. They might have come, perhaps, if it was a Tuesday or Friday.

He brought the remaining tubers up and kept them in a corner. He climbed on to the hammock and lay down on his side. With the roots fading in the dark, he felt as though he was suspended in the air. He lay completely still, without stirring the hammock even slightly, in order to catch any sound from below.

Ayya returned very late. Chidambaram had spotted Ayya when he was still far away. Ayya looked all around the banyan tree first. Then he stood at the entrance in the compound wall and listened. He came to the bank, climbed on to the temple's terrace and peeped in. He glanced in the direction of the bank. When his search was over, he stooped forward from the terrace and was about to step on to the compound wall. Chidambaram called from the hammock, 'I am here.'

He got down from the hammock.

'Why, you made me look everywhere and gave me a scare, son. Is that a place to lie down? What if the rope comes loose?'

'It's bound tight – won't come loose so easily.'

'Good job, son.'

They sat in a corner of the terrace. Ayya showed no signs of fatigue.

'You've come back so soon.'

'Yes, I have, somehow. Never mind. Did you have something to eat in the afternoon?'

'Oh, I ate well. I've kept your share.'

He brought the tubers and a piece of palm sugar, and gave them to his father.

'What a fine meal. Where did you find them?'

'Early tubers. I picked them.'

'So clever of you.'

Ayya split the tubers into pieces and ate them.

'I've brought some rice for you. Eat as much as you want.'

'Aren't you eating?'

'I've eaten already.'

'Let's eat together.'

'I can't eat more than this.'

Chidambaram finished his meal. Then they climbed down to the bank, washed their hands and climbed up again.

'This is such a good place. We'll sleep here. No need to bother getting inside the temple.'

'I thought so too.'

They spread their towels.

Ayya lit a bidi. He stubbed it out immediately and threw it away. Then he lay down on his back. Chidambaram lay on his side, watching Ayya. In the banyan tree, moaning sounds like a little child whining rose and faded every now and then.

'What happened with your work?' he asked.

'He gave me the money.'

'Have we sold all our goats?'

'He sold them using Mama's name. I told Aaththa yesterday.'

'What's an asset worth if it doesn't come handy in an emergency? Did you meet Mama today?'

'Yesterday was the last time I spoke to him.'

'Did you go to our village?'

'I didn't go in. We sat below the barren rock in the foothill and talked. The village headman and five others had come along with Mama.'

'What did they say?'

'What would they say? Don't wander around like this; just surrender, they told me. But we need someone to take up the case and fight, I said. Can you fight the case while you are in hiding, the headman asked me.'

'Are they asking us to surrender immediately?'

'Tomorrow.'

'In our village?'

'There is no court there. We have to surrender in a court. If we surrender in a police station, they'll boast that they captured us after a big manhunt. They'll take us to jail in handcuffs.'

'Why should they put handcuffs on us? Do they think we will escape and run away? If we want to escape, why would we go and surrender on our own?'

'They would like to pretend before the public that they captured us.'

'That's why I say, come what may, we should continue to hide. Let them find us. Let them catch us and put us in handcuffs.'

'But our family will be adrift until that happens.'

'If Vadakkuraan had caught me that day, my life would have been over, just like that. Imagine that it has actually happened. Imagine that your younger son too has died. Let's see if any policeman dares to come and catch me. I'll keep a stock of handmade bombs and throw them at all those who come after me. I'll bring them down like crows and sparrows, you'll see.'

'Do you think we will stay alive after losing you? Once we get you married, I'll have no worries. Then I can decide what suits me. I kept putting off everything because of that one reason. And now you're talking like this to me . . .'

'I have to get married too? You're always talking like this. Where do we have to present ourselves tomorrow?'

'In the neighbouring village.'

'Is it close by?'

'If we cross the tank and get on to the road, we can get a direct bus to go there.'

'Have you made arrangements?'

'I've fixed things with Mama. He'll come there with Aththai tomorrow. Chinnayya will come too, bringing your mother with him. If we reach there by ten, we can meet and chat with everyone; when the court staff arrive at eleven, we can go inside.'

'What do we do if some policemen from our village are in the court compound?'

'Our men will be there. They'll check regularly and let us know. Mama will stay put there.'

'Do we go directly from the court to jail?'

'Yes, the magistrate will take us from there. Straight to jail.'

'Will the magistrate ask us about anything?'

'He will say, what's the problem? We have to tell him what happened.'

'I'll tell him exactly what happened. What will you say?'

Ayya turned over on his side. He bent one arm at the elbow to support his head.

'I'll say I killed him.'

'So, both of us killed the same man. Won't the magistrate laugh at us?'

'You must say that you didn't kill him.'

'Should I lie, then?'

'If I confess, it ends with me. We can leave you out from the case. If they use a thousand lies to build the case, we also have to lie for our own good. That's our strategy.'

'You want to confess to something you never did and get arrested. Is that your strategy? Tell me now. If you are going to confess like that, I am not coming with you. I will kill the rest of them and come in later. Or I may just go into hiding and never turn up at all.'

'All right. Go ahead and confess, son. He will ask you why you killed him. What will you say?'

'I'll say, he killed my brother and so I killed him.'

'What if he asks whether anybody pushed you into doing it?'

'If I ask the judge who had pushed Vadakkuraan, what will he say?'

'What's he going to say? He is just going to write down our statements.'

'Let him write them down, then.'

'When the case is tried, only what you've said in court will stand.'

'So be it.'

'Our case will be lost. If we are not smart, he'll punish us.'

'Of course he will punish us. So, is it a smart move to surrender?'

'It's not like that, son. You are the one who killed him. Why have they included me as an accused? That's definitely a lie. We have to make a move to counter theirs.'

'I am going to admit in the court itself. Then their fraud will be exposed.'

'If you admit to the crime, they should release me, right?'

'Yes, if they are fair.'

'Do you think they will let me off so easily? They will get witnesses to lie in court and find a way to send me to prison. The same judge will award punishment for that, too.'

'Then why do we need a court? Is the court meant for punishing people through lies?'

'Do you know how many people are in jail for things they never did? The real criminals can bribe the officers and come out.'

'But should we let a judge who hands out unjust punishment survive? Instead of going to jail for something we never did, we can make his head roll right there, and go to jail for that.'

'The judge sits inside the court and conducts his enquiries only with those who come to him. Instead, he should go to the crime spot and talk to a few people there. He will come to know the truth only then. But he will do his work only in the court, give adjournment after adjournment, and drag on the case for years. For each adjournment, the court orderly has to shout for this one and that one to come forward, and he will demand money every time. You can go in only after you've paid a bribe at the entrance, thinking that you'll get justice there. Since all of them have come together to put up this farce, it can't be for free, right? Useless, jobless people. If you ask me, there should be no court. If someone does something bad, others should come together and punish him on the spot.'

'That ginning factory owner shot that man dead in front of so many people. Who punished him?'

'What can people do with only a cart driver's stick in their hands? Remember those fellows who marched in front that day, screaming their lungs out? They are the ones to blame. The same guys will be in front again when the murdered man's corpse is carried along the streets. Vile bastards!'

'Gang of thieves!'

'I told you, didn't I? We should also become clever like them.'

'Are you telling me to lie?'

Ayya lay down on his back again, with his knees raised and feet drawn in.

'When the situation demands, you have to say it.'

'Say what, exactly?'

'That you didn't kill him. That a young boy like you doesn't even know how to hold a sickle, so how would you dare to kill someone.'

'If he asks you?'

'I'll say I have nothing to do with that murder.'

'Supposing he asks you why, if there is no connection, you should come here and surrender, instead of staying at home?'

'The police had come to our house looking for us when we were not at home. So we got scared and took off from the village. We thought that our names might have been included.'

'Do we have to fight the case? What will happen then?'

'The case won't stand. Since the murder happened in the dark, they don't have a strong case. They will try to use witnesses to make it strong. The people on our street will handle those who are going to testify. They have all agreed on the same story. Mama would have got hold of a good lawyer by now. He will make every effort to get us out on bail. Once we are out, we have to fight the case and win, that's all. If we win the case, we'll be free forever.'

'If we are not set free?'

'Then jail will be our lot.'

'So we have to spend money and fight the case for that?'

'We have to see who wins, don't we?'

'Yeah, let's see.'

He felt an itch at the back of his throat. He tried to suppress the cough. Ayya turned to him.

'Why are you coughing so hard, son? You have such a bad cold. If the phlegm reaches your chest, the cough will get worse. You've got it from drinking water from all kinds of places. On top of that, you were not eating at the proper time. Do you have a headache?'

'It's only a slight cold.'

'If your health is so bad here, how will you manage in jail, eating that terrible food? It's not your fault. I should beat my head with a sandal.'

'Why? What's happened now?'

'Nothing. Sleep well. We shouldn't go there feeling drowsy because we didn't have proper sleep. Whatever be our troubles, we should be fully prepared to face them. Don't spoil your sleep unnecessarily. No one is going to come this way even after sunrise. We can sleep soundly and wake up whenever we want.'

Ayya didn't speak further. He sighed a couple of times.

Chidambaram lay down to sleep. His limbs were tired. Fatigue usually brought sound sleep.

8

The banyan tree had emptied of birds long before they woke up. After finishing their morning chores, they swam and bathed in the tank till their fatigue melted away. Taking dips in the water soothed the burning sensation in Chidambaram's eyes.

With a wet towel around the waist, they prostrated themselves thrice in front of the temple and offered their prayers. Picking up a handful of earth at the entrance, they smeared it on their foreheads. Once they got dressed, they headed towards the road, drying their towels in the breeze as they walked.

They could reach the main road by walking along the edge of the tank. Since harvesting in the area was still not over, the narrow trail leading to the road was in a poor condition. They found suitable detours and made progress.

Walking behind his father, Chidambaram suggested, 'Shall we walk on the road?'

Ayya turned. The hair on his head had become a tangle of black and grey.

'If we try to walk it there, we'll get delayed. We'll take the bus. It will be a short trip. Mama and Aththai will be waiting there along with the others.'

'Will Aaththa reach by then?'

'She has a direct bus. Chinnayya will bring her there.'

'Chiththi too?'

'She wanted to come, but there is the baby; so I told her not to come.'

'We can send back Aaththa with Mama.'

'Yes, we should.'

'I wonder how the dog is coping. It must have become thin. If you tie it up, the poor dog will keep whining. I don't think Aththai will let it grow thin.'

'If Aaththa is around, the dog will feel better.'

'It will play happily with Thangachi.'

'I wonder if the police has wrecked the house. It will need a lot of repair.'

'If they couldn't catch us, why damage the house?'

When they saw two people in a field, they stopped talking and walked faster. After passing them, Ayya asked him, 'Did you wash your shirt and dhoti? They look clean.'

'I washed them with soap yesterday.'

'Aththai will bring our clothes. We'll get dressed and have something to eat. Then we can go directly to the court.'

'Do we have to eat in a food stall?'

'Do you think your aththai will let us? She would have prepared and brought food for us.'

'If both of us go in together, won't they suspect us?'

'We should enter as if we don't know each other. We mustn't stop no matter who gets in the way. If they catch us, the police will claim that we were captured on the hillside. After hiding for so long, we can't fall into their hands.'

'We are getting caught deliberately. How does it matter who has caught us?'

'But we aren't getting caught out of stupidity!'

Ayya stopped. 'Yes. We know what we are doing. Keep moving. I'll come out of jail. Their heads will roll on the ground in front of the temple.'

'Let's come out first.'

The road was quite near. The traffic of vehicles was clearly visible. He moved closer to his father.

'Where do I keep the weapons?'

'Give them to Mama. He will carry them home.'

'We must ask him to hone the sickle properly and keep it ready.'

A bus was approaching from the north.

'See that bus? Come. Let's make a run for it.'

Ayya started running.

Clutching his weapons carefully, Chidambaram ran behind Ayya.

Afterword

I remember my teenage years vividly each time I return to my novel *Heat*. Chidambaram, on whom I had inflicted the torment of wandering endlessly across hills and plains, is my doorway to these memories.

The boy's world is like a garden sheltered by the cool shade of affection. He plays with his little cousin, is loved by his aunt, defended by father and uncle, protected by his mother and showered with affection by his brother and sister. He is engulfed in a world of delight.

Suddenly one day Janaki, cousin and inseparable friend, catches fever and dies. He turns into a beetle whose wings are broken. He refuses to go to school without her. His loving brother becomes the victim of a powerful man's rapacious greed. The murder shatters the family.

His tender heart, which has always bristled at the world's cruelties, turns into a furnace. Instead of his schoolbag, he picks up a sickle. Though the father harbours a thirst for revenge, it's the son who confronts the enemy first. In a surprising twist, the enemy is killed.

At an age when boys like him should lead a carefree life, he is forced to live as a fugitive, wandering through forests and hills, drenched cold by the rain, haunted every moment by memories of home. Protective of the boy like a mother hen, the father is worried about his only remaining son's future.

'Will there be no end to a world where the strong prey on the weak?' A million such questions arise in the boy's troubled mind. The fearless boy refuses to surrender. A mother's affection calms his stormy heart. Dreaming bitterly of a distant dawn, the boy follows his father into the darkness of a life in prison.

Yes, this is a children's story. It is a searing tale of a young firebird that dared to look at life's contradictions in the face and for a way to resolve them.

The murder in *Heat* actually happened. Like a tender shoot ravaged by insects, the young boy had to face many trials. I wanted to write a novel knitting the idyllic world of a young boy with the raging heat of his mind. Blending my boyhood experiences of grazing goats and cattle, hunting, playing and wandering across hills, graveyards, temples and tanks with the incidents around the murder, I became Chidambaram. He was the killer; I was the one who went into hiding and roamed the forest.

For helping, even if belatedly, Chidambaram's passage into the portals of another language, my heartfelt gratitude to my friend and translator Kalyan Raman.

Poomani
Kovilpatti

Translator's Note

This novel is unusual in many ways. It has a simple storyline, based on a real-life incident. A fifteen-year-old boy kills a man. Then he goes into hiding with his father in the forests and hills near his home town. They spend a week surviving in the wilderness under harsh conditions before they eventually surrender to the police.

During their life as outlaws, father and son spend their time in a variety of locations: forested tank bed, rocky outcrop, graveyard, temple and cane field, among others. They forage for food, cook, clean, endure hunger and thirst, scout for locations, trudge very long distances over hills and plains and also, in the case of the boy, find ways to amuse themselves with diversions. They also reminisce, together and alone, about the past, the incidents that sowed enmity in the boy's heart and led to the murder.

Vekkai, the Tamil original of *Heat*, has earned a special place in the canon of modernist Tamil literature of the twentieth century. It is the second of two landmark novels with a subaltern backdrop that Poomani, now a distinguished elder of Tamil letters, wrote in his early thirties. Both for the poignant story it tells and for its exemplary craft, the novel won wide critical acclaim at the time of first publication and has been regarded ever since as a classic. A thirtieth-anniversary edition was published in 2012, ensuring that this special work, which has remained fresh and original even after so many years, will be available to younger readers in the years to come. *Vekkai* is also the first of Poomani's novels to be translated into English.

What makes *Heat* unusual is the extraordinary humanity with which the author brings alive the world of low-caste, poor Tamils. The novel does not reduce the boy's family to victims of oppression who belong to this or that caste. They have their battles with landlords and their henchmen, factory owners and commission agents, the police, politicians, the illicit liquor business and the courts of justice. And yes, it is these events that form the plot of the story.

But the novel sets the politics in the background,

essentializing it in many respects, and draws instead an extraordinary cast of characters – complex, tender, written with real empathy – and their relationships with one another. Since very few novels of the subaltern life had been written in the naturalist mode at the time, Poomani had to invent a language along with the story that brought real life closer to literary fiction.

The prose is economical – yet the brief, pregnant exchanges between the individuals lend a vivid and vital shape to each character. A few details evoke a whole landscape. Small shifts of wind, light and a few leaves on the trees set the mood for a situation. And there is love. The eminent Tamil writer B. Jeyamohan observed once that a fine thread of love runs through every page of this novel. Familial love – between father and son, siblings, aunt and nephew, cousins, sisters-in-law – is expressed in countless ways in every situation in the narrative, through attention, touch, empathy, gesture and play.

As the translator I have tried hard to reproduce the evocative magic of Poomani's narrative style and language. Inevitably, there are challenges. The idioms and phrases that arise from the life lived in the region where the novel is set could not always travel smoothly to English. Some plants and vegetation local to the area were given their formal botanical names that will not be easily recognized by readers of the English text. Beyond these constraints, there is enough in the translator's art, one hopes, to bring the story and people of *Heat* alive in a new language.

I thank R. Sivapriya and Chiki Sarkar of Juggernaut Books for commissioning the translation and ably transforming the text through the editing and production process into a splendid volume. I am grateful to the author Poomani for the gift and grace of his friendship, which has played no small part in inspiring and enhancing the quality of this work.

N. Kalyan Raman
Chennai

juggernaut

THE APP
FOR INDIAN
READERS

*Fresh, original books tailored for
mobile and for India. Starting at ₹10.*

juggernaut.in

1

CRAFTED FOR MOBILE READING

Thought you would never read a book on mobile? Let us prove you wrong.

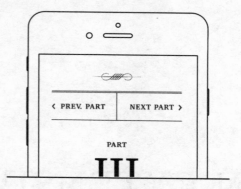

Beautiful Typography

The quality of print transferred
to your mobile. Forget ugly PDFs.

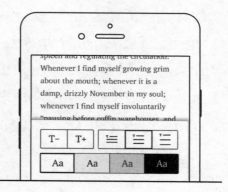

Customizable Reading

Read in the font size, spacing
and background of your liking.

AN EXTENSIVE LIBRARY

Including fresh, new, original Juggernaut books from the likes of Sunny Leone, Praveen Swami, Husain Haqqani, Umera Ahmed, Rujuta Diwekar and lots more. Plus, books from partner publishers and loads of free classics. Whichever genre you like, there's a book waiting for you.

DON'T JUST READ; INTERACT

We're changing the reading experience from passive to active.

Ask authors questions

Get all your answers from the horse's mouth. Juggernaut authors actually reply to every question they can.

Rate and review

Let everyone know of your favourite reads or critique the finer points of a book – you will be heard in a community of like-minded readers.

Gift books to friends

For a book-lover, there's no nicer gift than a book personally picked. You can even do it anonymously if you like.

Enjoy new book formats

Discover serials released in parts over time, picture books including comics, and story-bundles at discounted rates. And coming soon, audiobooks.

4

LOWEST PRICES & ONE-TAP BUYING

Books start at ₹10 with regular discounts and free previews.

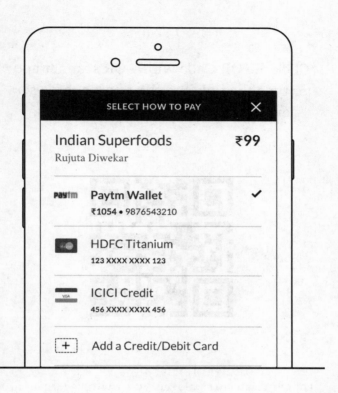

Paytm Wallet, Cards & Apple Payments

On Android, just add a Paytm Wallet once and buy any book with one tap. On iOS, pay with one tap with your iTunes-linked debit/credit card.

Click the QR Code with a QR scanner app
or type the link into the Internet browser
on your phone to download the app.

For our complete catalogue, visit www.juggernaut.in
To submit your book, send a synopsis and two
sample chapters to books@juggernaut.in
For all other queries, write to contact@juggernaut.in